Jam[...]

MEL

PUG
LIFE

daisy

Jenners

HENRIK

JAMIE McFLAIR
VS THE
ULTIMATE BRAIN HACK

ALSO BY LUKE FRANKS & SEAN THORNE

Jamie McFlair Vs The Boyband Generator

JAMIE McFLAIR VS THE ULTIMATE BRAIN HACK

LUKE & SEAN
FRANKS THORNE

ILLUSTRATED BY DAVIDE ORTU

HODDER CHILDREN'S BOOKS

First published in Great Britain in 2022 by Hodder & Stoughton

1 3 5 7 9 10 8 6 4 2

A CIP catalogue record for this book
is available from the British Library.

ISBN 978 1 444 95604 7

Typeset by Avon DataSet Ltd, Arden Court, Alcester, Warwickshire

Printed and bound in Great Britain by Clays Ltd, Elcograf S.p.A.

The paper and board used in this book
are made from wood from responsible sources.

Hodder Children's Books
An imprint of
Hachette Children's Group
Part of Hodder & Stoughton Limited
Carmelite House
50 Victoria Embankment
London EC4Y 0DZ

An Hachette UK Company
www.hachette.co.uk

www.hachettechildrens.co.uk

**THIS BOOK IS DEDICATED TO YOU! YES YOU!
THE FACT YOU'VE COME BACK TO JOIN JAMIE FOR
A SECOND ADVENTURE GENUINELY MEANS THE WORLD
TO US AND WE HOPE YOU HAVE A LOVELY TIME!**

CHAPTER 1
THE ROFLCOPTER

It was 11 a.m. on a cold February morning when Barry Bigtime's alarm began to screech. Once upon a time, Barry would have woken up in a luxurious four-poster bed but now he was crammed into the back of a small helicopter with his undesirable roommates, Slottapuss and Flobster. The helicopter brimmed with sad smells. As Barry opened his eyes, Flobster's ghastly face was only inches away from his own. He sat up with a start. If you've ever been annoyed at sharing a bedroom with a brother or sister, Barry Bigtime could assure you things could be **MUCH WORSE.** You could be sleeping alongside a six-foot rodent with human limbs and a half-man, half-lobster who smelt as bad as he looked.

Only three months ago, Barry had been one of the most influential and affluent men not only in the world of music, but in the whole world of humans. He'd wake up in his beautiful mansion where fresh, deep-fried penguin wings would be served to him by one of his many household staff, fuelling him for a day of dominating the music industry.

Barry's life came crashing down around him when he created a boyband (in his Boyband Generator) that turned into a **MONSTER AT A MUSIC FESTIVAL.** Barry had been on the run with his two henchthings ever since. The whole sordid affair is documented in a book called *Jamie McFlair vs The Boyband Generator*. It really is a **WILD** tale.

As Barry struggled to sit up, he locked eyes with a photograph of Jamie McFlair that he'd torn out of a newspaper and nailed to a dartboard. Her smiling face was peppered with tiny holes. In Barry's mind, his niece had been solely responsible for the downfall of his music empire. It was her fault that he now had to live in a helicopter with rat-people and lobster-men. It was her fault he'd had to spend the last month hiding from Detective Lansdown on a deserted island (which, we hasten to add, wasn't one of those tropical deserted islands but a weird, cold, blustery one off the coast of Scotland).

It was her fault that Barry Bigtime had lost . . . well, essentially everything. **'She will pay!'** Barry snarled. With no more darts to hand, he picked up a shrivelled easy-peeler orange and hurled it at the dartboard. It jammed on to a dart and sprayed a sleeping Slottapuss with orange goo.

Slottapuss's long, rat-like muzzle crinkled. He shuffled under the blanket he'd fashioned out of papers covered with Barry's crazy drawings and mad plans. **'GET UP, YOU TWO. TODAY IS THE DAY,'** Barry shouted with unnecessary volume. He switched the lights on (they weren't really lights but four torches gaffer-taped together). The beams shone directly into Flobster's eyes. His antennae twitched with shock, his long human arms waggled and his under-the-sea claws clicked as he writhed in the nest he'd made out of newspaper.

Barry was already on his feet and whipped away Slottapuss's blanket of plans. The former showbiz

kingpin shuffled awkwardly to the front of the helicopter and spread the papers over the cockpit.

As well as being a musical genius, Barry was also an **ACTUAL GENIUS.** Some would say he was also an evil genius. A tri-genius, if you will. His Boyband Generator could infuse superstar talent into human brains. You might think that Barry created this to make some great music, but, while some of his creations did make some toe-tapping tunes, the *real* reason Barry built the Boyband Generator was for fame, fortune and, most importantly, **POWER.**

With all of that now in the past and in the papers, Barry had been frantically designing a new machine. One that made the Boyband Generator look like one of those old phones that only had one game.

Barry's crazed eyes studied the plans one last time.

'DID YOU GET THE BIRTHDAY CARD LIKE I ASKED?' he yelled.

'Yes,' grumbled Slottapuss. 'I got it when I bought those oranges and almost scared the lady half to death, remember?'

The island they'd been hiding on was completely deserted, apart from one village that felt like it had been frozen sixty years in the past. The islanders hadn't discovered the internet, 5G, or even national newspapers, so nobody knew who Barry was. Which was ideal, because his face was **PLASTERED ON THE FRONT OF HIS HELICOPTER.**

'Are there any oranges left?' asked Flobster. 'I'm starving.'

'You can eat when I've got the funds I need to build our **new machine,**' barked Barry. 'And all the other delights that our plan requires . . .' *What a plan this is*, he thought. If this new machine design worked, Barry could become more powerful than ever. It would make him rich again. It would restore his besmirched name. Best of all, it would also **DEAL WITH THAT BRAT, JAMIE MCFLAIR.**

CHAPTER 2

THE ORDER OF MEGACLEESE

'So to be clear, we definitely weren't invited to the party?' said Slottapuss from the pilot's seat.

'Of course not. Gregorius Megacleese is one of the most powerful men in the **ENTIRE** world. There is just one invitation and it's mine!'

Barry held the invitation aloft and read aloud. '"To Barry Bigtime". See, that's all it says, just Barry there, look. **Just Me.** Ahem. "As a member of the Order of Megacleese, you are cordially invited, along with other order members, to celebrate my fiftieth birthday at my private island estate. Do RSVP by 8 August . . . Gregorius. PS Free food and drink."'

'Just so I'm clear . . . **What is the Order of Megacleese, again?'** asked Flobster. The lobster-man was stroking his dangly antennae with the smooth side of his lobster claws. His apron was covered with mysterious juices.

Barry rolled his eyes. 'How many times do I need to go over this with you two schmucks? You know what it is! We formed it at Billy Clarkson's sixtieth birthday party at my chateau, after Gerry Fredericks won the limbo. It's an exclusive order of the richest and most powerful people in the world. They'll all be at Gregorius's birthday party. A perfect time for me to acquire the resources I need to build my new machine . . .'

Flobster and Slottapuss both nodded, silently begging their **HIDEOUS BRAINS** to absorb every word to avoid a future scolding.

'And what is your most important task?' said Barry.

'Hold our position,' said Slottapuss and Flobster almost in unison but not quite.

'Unless you send us the signal,' added Flobster.

'And what's the signal?' asked Barry.

'A poop and a fan emoji,' recited Slottapuss.

'Precisely,' said Barry.

'And you're sure this Gregorius isn't a sneaky, telltale snitch?' asked Slottapuss. 'He's definitely not going to call Detective Lansdown as soon as he sees you?'

'Gregorius and I have been friends for many years. I got him out of a few sticky situations back in our youth. Plus, *The Big Time*'s TV ratings made Gregorius the most successful head of the Hun TV network of all time,' said Barry. 'Besides, the Order is a sacred bond of finance and friendship. **Nobody is going to snitch.'**

Slottapuss highly doubted the loyalty of a club that was formed during limbo-victory jubilation, but he didn't dare share that with anyone.

'I see the island,' yelled Slottapuss and, sure enough, Gregorius's private island estate came into view.

'I see the house!' exclaimed Flobster.

'It's even bigger than yours, boss!' added Slottapuss.

'Well, technically it's not his any more because—'

'SILENCE, GROTSACKS,' shouted Barry, half annoyed at the hollering and half annoyed at the fact that Gregorius's house was bigger than his lovely old chateau, with its lovely gardens, marshmallow room and private pizza restau— Nope, these thoughts were unhelpful. If Barry was going to secure these resources, he needed to focus and put on the performance of a lifetime.

'Be careful parking the roflcopter, Slotty. Don't scratch anyone else's aircraft,' Barry said nervously as they lowered into Gregorius's helicopter parking zone . . . Nervousness was a very new brain sensation for Barry. He didn't like it one bit. *The last time I felt like this was when I would arrive at school and Big Lobber and his crew would spot me and—*

This memory was thankfully interrupted as Slottapuss brought the roflcopter down with a slightly uncomfortable jolt. But to be fair, Slottapuss had done some solid helicoptering throughout, **SO WELL DONE HIM.** Barry stepped out into the brisk breeze, filling his lungs with delicious fresh air. He spruced himself up in the reflection of the helicopter glass and turned to Slottapuss and Flobster.

'How do I look?' he asked.

The two beasts looked at each other. They would never say it, but we will. **BARRY WAS A SHAMBLES.** His once shiny, action-figure skin was now pink and blotchy. His once gleaming eyes were dull and tired. His usually perfectly slicked-back hair was tousled and speckled with shoots of grey. A two-month diet of eating weird, remote-island takeaways had made his belly bulbous and his jowls saggy. His polar bear fur coat still looked on point, though.

'Yeah, you look great, boss.'

'Yeah, that look is fire,' came the desperate replies.

'Brilliant. Now remember. Hold your positions, unless I give you the signal,' said Barry. 'When we leave this island, Barry Bigtime will be back with a vengeance.'

CHAPTER 3

THE DIAMOND ROOM

Barry strode towards the red-brick Megacleese estate. He scrunched his nose at the lack of embellishments – a world away from his once flamboyant decor. There wasn't even a **SINGLE STATUE OF GREGORIUS** in sight.

The front door was guarded by two strong-looking men who looked like leathery baked potatoes with arms and legs.

'Can I see your invitation, sir?' said Old Potato Man.

Barry gasped. **'Are you serious?** I'm Barry Bigtime!'

Bald Potato chuckled, his head glistening in the winter sun.

'Ah, Mr Bigtime, I'm afraid I have bad news,' Bald said, in a tone that Barry was not accustomed to. 'Your invitation has been withdrawn, mate. Mr Megacleese forwards his apologies.'

A **FIERY RAGE** bubbled in the pit of Barry's tummy and he felt his face redden. *'Mate'? Who do they think they are talking to?*

'Listen here, humpty,' snarled Barry. 'If you don't let me past, I will make sure Gregorius hears of this, and I will personally make sure to airlift you two schlubs back to a body of water of MY choosing where you will then be fed to a **snarling, snapping shark of the hungry variety!'**

Old and Bald burst out laughing. 'Think you'll have a hard job doing that after a little girl stole your house!' Old mocked.

'Come on, mate. Sling your hook and we won't have a little birdie tell the coppers where you're hiding,' added Bald.

Barry turned and stormed off, heading towards the side of the house. He *needed* to get into the estate. Or his plan was already dead. There must be some mistake. Gregorius wouldn't uninvite him to a birthday party.

That only happens at eleven-year-olds' birthday parties. OK, it had happened a little too often for young Barry, but that was long ago.

He ignored the shouts of, 'That's not the way back to the helicopter parking zone, Mr Bigtime,' and, 'Don't make us have to come get you.' *There has to be some sort of entrance around the side. Something unguarded, like an open window . . . drainage . . . ventilation . . .*

Barry's thoughts were interrupted by the sound of leather potato men trying to run. What proceeded to take place was the **SLOWEST CHASE** in the history of chases. None of these three men had any right to be involved in a chase. Nevertheless, the chase was on. Old and Bald were heaving and wheezing in their leathers as Barry puffed and panted in the sweaty furs of his polar bear coat.

As Barry ran, he noticed a door, next to which was what looked like a cat flap. But larger. *Does Gregorius have the biggest cats in the world?* Barry suddenly remembered Gregorius was fond of a much more reptilian and **DANGEROUS TOOTHY BEAST.** The fact that Barry had time to think all these things and still not be that close to the big flap gives you an idea of the pace of this chase. At this point, we're just filling for time until he gets to the big flap. It's such a slow chase. Let's skip to the bit when he gets there . . .

Barry reached the big flap. Old and Bald were still a comfortable distance away and would have no chance of squeezing through such an opening. Barry dropped down and **SLID LIKE A SLUG THROUGH THE BIG FLAP** (which was still quite a tight fit). 'Come on,' growled Barry. *I can't be stuck.* He frantically tried to wriggle himself through the gap, but he was stuck fast. The footsteps and the wheezes of Old and Bald grew closer. There was a click and a creak and the door next to the flap swung open as the potatoes plodded inside.

'What's happened here, then?' asked Old with a smirk.

'Didn't fancy using the door?' added Bald.

Barry, who had absolutely no answer to this question, released some pungent anger words followed by some pungent bottom smells.

'Well, you're in big trouble now,' said Old, grimacing. 'My Mrs has made me watch that *Big Time* rubbish for years, and I've always wanted to do this . . .'

He drew back his fist. But before this knuckle sandwich could reach Barry's chops, a loud voice echoed around the kitchen.

'**Ksssht.** Could you bring Mr Bigtime from the kitchen into the dining hall, please. We've just seen the three of you waddle past our window.'

It was the voice of Gregorius Megacleese.

*

Old and Bald marched Barry into the dining hall, where at the end of a long table sat Gregorius Megacleese, head of the Hun Entertainment & News network and **THE THIRD RICHEST MAN** in the whole of the solar system. He had thin wisps of fair hair and glasses with lenses so tiny it was hard to see the point of them. He was wearing a black turtleneck and an equally black blazer. On his shoulder, however, was a plume of colour – **A MECHANICAL PARROT** shimmering from blue to gold. Gregorius, like Barry, had always had a strange affinity with animals. The parrot squawked on Barry's arrival.

'*Bwark*. Barry-Not-So-Bigtime. *Bwark*. Uh-oh. Uh-oh. *Bwark*.'

Chuckles filled the room.

Barry's eyes darted through the guests surrounding the table, each of them the kingpins of the entertainment industry. The stench of money was thick in the air. Some faces he recognised, like the queen of book publishing, Hilda McKaren; the owner of the Super Awesome Actors' Dominion, Fredericksen Hansen Christiansen Pedersen Smith; and the duke of radio, a man who just went by the name of **TWINKLE.** There were many he didn't recognise. But he didn't like the way they were looking at him.

'I uninvited you. Yet you are here anyway,' said Gregorius. His voice was quiet and dangerous. **'Maybe I should invest in better security?'**

Old and Bald gulped and dropped their gaze.

'Uninvite me . . . But why, Gregorius, we are dear friends!' said Barry in a voice that seemed calm, but the pulsating veins on his head suggested otherwise.

Gregorius rolled his eyes and shook his head as the parrot hopped into his hand.

'Barry, you are a wanted man. You created four monsters in your laboratory and unleashed them on to a music festival,' said Gregorius, calm and cold. 'In what world would you still be welcome at an occasion such as this?'

Barry felt his **RAGE** oven start to warm. It was important to stay calm.

'Now hang on, that wasn't my fault. I didn't mean for them to be boyband monsters!' Barry said. Guffaws echoed throughout the dining hall.

'Don't try and hoodwink a man who has known you for over fifty years,' said Gregorius. 'I warned you about the Boyband Generator. You wouldn't listen to me back then but maybe you'll listen to me now. **Leave.** I'm giving you this chance to go back to wherever you were hiding. Gentlemen, escort Mr Bigtime—'

'NO, wait!' yelled Barry. He pulled himself from Old and Bald's grip and slammed his hands on to the table.

'You'll want to hear what I have to say. I've got

something here that's huge. Bigger than the Boyband Generator. It will ensure the Order of Megacleese stays in power for ever. **We'll ALL be rich. Richer than we already are.'**

Some of the other guests were beginning to lose patience.

'My caviar's getting stagnant,' someone whined.

'My eyes are saddened by this man's appearance,' hollered someone else.

'He isn't even rich any more!' complained another.

Gregorius raised a hand and silence fell. 'Because you're an old friend, Barry, I'll let you talk. But as soon as Beakers here gets bored, I'm afraid your time will be up.'

'*Bwark*. I'm all ears. *Bwark*,' came the cry from Beakers, the mechanical parrot.

Barry closed his eyes. He couldn't mess this up. His rage oven was beginning to overheat. He summoned all of his poise.

'Gregorius, my friend, I understand the Boyband Generator had its flaws. But you'll be pleased to know I've solved them. My new machine could theoretically work anywhere! And it would give us full control of the subject's **ENTIRE BRAIN** . . . and they would be powerless to resist. All the subjects would be controlled from one console, wherever they are in the world!'

A few murmurs of interest started to bubble around the dining table. Barry's Bigtime-ness was starting to flood back into his brain.

With the glimmer back in his eye, he brandished his dastardly plans that he had scribbled down during his two months in hiding. With every word he could feel each money-hungry face gravitate closer as his plan spelt out big bucks for all.

'And we found the perfect location. I found it during my time island-hopping. I'll disclose its location once I have your support, but I tell you, it's perfect. The plan I've spelt out to you **CANNOT FAIL.** I suggest we start this September. That gives us seven months to get everything ready, which with our collective resources is completely achievable. If, of course, you're on board. Gregorius, old friend?'

The Order exchanged murmurs and their eyes turned to Gregorius, who had listened intently.

'Well . . .' said Gregorius. He paused. 'This all sounds very good to me, Barry.'

Barry's brain began to pump out happiness chemicals for the first time in months.

'I don't doubt the science. I don't doubt the plan,' Gregorius added, rising to his feet. **'I just doubt you.'**

The warm and toasty happiness chemicals turned into scorched crumbs of shame.

'Wh-what?' stammered Barry.

'The resources to run this would be what, forty . . . fifty . . . maybe a hundred million pounds? At least? Why would I trust that to a man who let a little girl steal his house and destroy his legacy?'

'Even a hundred million is a drop in the ocean to you, Gregorius. Do you still have that entirely diamond-encrusted room, by the way?'

'I've got four diamond rooms now, Barry, thanks for asking. Do you know why I now have four? Because I am not reckless. I am not wasteful. I am not stupid.' Gregorius's voice was rising, but Barry had to stand firm.

'I am the only man on earth who knows how to use this technology. I am the only person who can build this new machine! I beg you, Gregorius, this is zero risk for you!' Barry said desperately.

'Beg,' spat Gregorius. 'Barry Bigtime begging for bullish bailouts because he's bankrupt and can't build his bonkers new blueprint . . .' The unnecessary alliteration caused an awkward silence. 'What have you become? Maybe I should let Rita and Mavis here put you out of your misery.' Gregorius gestured behind him. Rising on to their hind legs were Gregorius's toothy reptile friends of the **SNAPPING** variety. Gregorius not only liked small, friendly robot animals, but much like Barry had Slottapuss and

Flobster, Gregorius had Rita and Mavis, two robotic, **HUMANOID CROCODILES**. They snapped their big jaws at Barry hungrily.

Barry gulped and his legs became wobbly, but he had one last card up his sleeve . . .

'One final thing! Here's your birthday card,' he said, flinging the purple envelope down on the table.

Gregorius opened the card. Inside were only six words and none of them were 'Happy birthday'.

Remember Lobber Livingstone.

Remember Farnell Winterbottom.

For the first time, Gregorius's hard expression wavered as he stared at the card. The two locked eyes for what became a slightly uncomfortable length of time.

'Finance and friendship, Gregorius, that was what the order was built on,' said Barry.

'Finance and friendship,' agreed Gregorius. 'Finance that you no longer have. Thank you for the card. As a token of appreciation, I will allow you to be thrown forcefully from this building rather than consumed. **Men, get rid of him.'**

And with that, Old and Bald grabbed Barry's arms, but not before Barry whipped out his phone to send poop and fan emojis.

'Time to take out the trash,' said Bald, like a cringe movie villain, as he slung the struggling Barry Bigtime on to the front drive. There was more **CRINGE** to come as the guards fist-bumped before they resumed their positions at the front door of the Megacleese estate.

Barry gingerly clambered to his feet and made a beeline back to the roflcopter. He checked his watch. *That was a long struggle. We have to leave as soon as possible.* He walked down the long, paved path towards the helicopter park, which was surrounded by tall and immaculately trimmed hedgerows. Once out of sight of Old and Bald, Barry ran as fast as he possibly could.

Flobster was waiting and the roflcopter's propellers had already begun to spin.

'Well?' shouted Barry over the helicopter's whir.

'Did it work?'

Flobster was wearing a black ski-mask, but his antennae were waggling happily and his pincers were clicking with excitement. 'Like a charm, sir. **We got the lot!**'

Barry jumped into the helicopter. Sitting in the pilot's seat, also wearing a ski-mask and leather gloves, was Slottapuss. Barry could see him grinning.

'Do you think this will be enough, boss?' said the rat, rolling up his mask and gesturing to the back of the roflcopter.

Barry's eyes almost launched out of his head and into space. What was once their grubby little sleeping den was now a treasure trove full to bursting with sacks and sacks of twinkling diamonds.

'In a pleasant surprise,' said Flobster, 'there were actually FOUR diamond rooms and not just the one like we thought!'

Barry was submerged in the loot, examining each diamond-encrusted trinket with eager eyes. There were **DIAMOND FRUIT BOWLS FILLED WITH DIAMOND BANANAS,** a diamond cheese grater and even diamond snooker balls.

'So, I'd say we got way more than what we needed,' added Slottapuss, examining a heavy, strange diamond pot filled with a dusty, gravelly mixture.

'This is tremendous work, my grubby friends,' said Barry, rubbing his hands together.

'Stealing all of this from one of your oldest friends was a stroke of genius,' said Slottapuss, snacking on the dry but delicious contents of the diamond pot.

'I gave Gregorius ample opportunity to help us voluntarily, but he's always needed me to know what's good for him. So we haven't stolen . . . we've just loaned this to ourselves! We'll pay Gregorius back once this plan makes me the most powerful man in the world. If anything, I've done Gregorius a favour.'

'Of course! We're not monsters!' replied Slottapuss with a mouth full of gravelly dust.

The rat-man, the lobster-man and the horrible man all laughed heartily for the first time in months. Operation Rubbslings had begun . . .

CHAPTER 4
THE BARON OF BRAMBLES

SIX MONTHS LATER

Jamie McFlair, aka Thunderflower, was wearing her Kid Ninja World Book Day costume, pointing a **BUBBLE BLASTER** at Jenners, who in this game was the evil Baron of Brambles. They were playing Flower Samurais of Death.

'*Let Daffodil Jill go, Brambles. I won't warn you or that BEAST again,*' Thunderflower yelled, swishing her long red hair.

Daffodil Jill, otherwise known as Mel, was wearing one of those novelty daffodil hats you get for Saint David's day or Welsh rugby games. She was hanging upside down in the paws of a very real fez-wearing bear who also had a pair of human ears (this fact is unrelated to the game but we thought worth mentioning). Henrik the bear, who in real life was **GENTLE AND CLUMSY,** was really committing to the role of villainous henchman far more than he'd ever done during his time as Barry Bigtime's actual villainous henchman

The bear gave a loud roar that crossed Daffodil Jill's eyes and left everyone's ears ringing.

'Henrik, you can't be too loud, you're still supposed to be a bit of a **secret!'** hissed Jamie, breaking character.

'Sorry!' said Henrik in a hushed voice, bringing a paw to his mouth.

'YOU'RE OUTNUMBERED, THUNDERFLOWER!' yelled the Baron of Brambles in an even louder roar than Henrik's. 'TIME TO GIVE UP THE FLOWER CRYSTALS OR SAY GOODBYE TO YOUR FRIENDS FOR EVER.' Her branches shook menacingly.

'Looks like someone is here to even up the odds,' came the voice of a new challenger.

Daisy leapt between Thunderflower and the Baron of Brambles. You'd be forgiven for thinking Daisy was dressed as a daisy. Especially if you've only just joined us for book two. For the rest of you, though, you'd know **DAISY WASN'T THAT BASIC.**

Daisy was wearing pink gardening gloves, a pointed green hat, and a Father Christmas beard. Daisy's character was Queen Gnome and, despite the absurdity of the garments, she was somehow managing to pull the look off.

'YOU ASKED FOR IT!' yelled Queen Gnome. Thunderflower and Queen Gnome whirled their arms in a synchronised motion and, with a flash of lightning and a crash of thunder, an army of gnomes shielded by bubbles of electricity were summoned from the kingdoms of Gnomeo Dunn.

'CHARGE!' yelled Queen Gnome, pointing a defiant pink finger at the bear.

The electrified gnomes overpowered the grizzly and Daffodil Jill escaped her captor, joining her friends with a triple backflip, quadruple somersault and a double waggling thumbs up.

'Game's up, Brambles,' shouted Thunderflower.

'Looks like we're going to have to cut you down to size,' added Queen Gnome.

'We're taking you downtown!' added Daffodil Jill, which sounded cool but didn't make much sense.

'Cut me down to size, EH?' yelled Brambles. 'Well, why not TRY THIS ON FOR SIZE?' Her roots dug into the grass of the Bramblewood, absorbing powerful, evil nutrients. As each nutrient sapped into her branches, the Baron of Brambles grew to be TRIPLE the size, which meant—

'Wait, does the Baron of Brambles have power of growth? Is that fair?' asked Daisy quickly.

'Yeah, she grew during a lunchtime in Year 5, I think,' replied Jamie.

'Yeah, I remember that, so she could **RIDE THE HIPPOS** of the valley,' said Mel.

'OK, just checking,' finished Daisy.

—which meant there was only one thing for it . . .

'FLOWER CRYSTALS ACTIVATE!'

The girls brandished their flower crystals containing their individual powers of 'Gnomes', 'Thunder' and

'Intense hay fever'. They connected them, combining their powers. Red, yellow and blue beams blasted into the Baron of Brambles, making her violently sneezy, overwhelmed by gnomes and also electrocuted, all at the same time. It was all too much. She sank to the ground with a loud, guttural roar.

'She should probably be dead for ever now,' mused Daisy, pointing at Jenners, who was still groaning and writhing.

With the Baron of Brambles **SMOULDERING** in the grass, Jamie felt a pang of sympathy. *What had made the Baron of Brambles so evil?* she wondered. It wasn't a storyline they were ever going to explore because Flower Samurais of Death had joined Fruitykins figures, Club Meerkat and StompyDog videos as fun times consigned permanently to the past. Jamie looked around at her best friends. Jenners spreadeagled on the floor in branches. Mel looking triumphant in her flower hat. Daisy still managing to look like a queen in gardening gloves and a Santa beard. She wanted to screenshot this sight and save it in her brain for ever and then remembered that her phone had that exact function, **CALLED A CAMERA.**

'We should probably get a picture of this!' said Jamie and assembled her friends for a selfie that ranked highly on the adorable chart. *This could be one of my all-time favourite photos*, thought Jamie, as everyone gave the universal 'ahhh' noise that signified a good photo had been taken.

It was the last week of summer, and Jamie, Jenners, Daisy and Mel had gathered in Jamie's massive garden for the final game of Flower Samurais of Death. Why was this the last EVER game? Well, for one, you can't play Flower Samurais of Death at big school, can you? That would be a **POOR LIFE CHOICE.** And for two (and more distressingly), Jamie, Jenners, Daisy and Mel were all going to different new secondary schools in September. And for Jamie this really did feel like the end of the world. Even though Jamie had faced the potential end of the world in the form of monster-fied boyband creatures, this rather more common problem for an almost twelve-year-old seemed just as scary. Of course, in reality, the girls could still see each other on Zoom or FaceTime and on weekends, but these rational explanations wouldn't settle in Jamie's brain. *I'll never find friends this good at stupid Crudwell High,* Jamie thought.

There was also one stubborn brain-stain that she couldn't shift. **THE THREAT OF HER EVIL UNCLE BARRY.**

'*You will pay dearly for this. I will tear down your house, just like I did your grandma's. I'll take everything you own, just like I did to your mother. I will make sure you, your friends and anyone you've ever cared about are miserable for the rest of their lives and there will be nothing you can do to stop that now, because I am Barry Bigtime.*' Those were the final words her uncle had whispered to her before disappearing on his helicopter last summer. They had echoed around Jamie's head ever since. Who would say that to their own niece?

He was still out there somewhere

and stewing that Jamie and her friends had destroyed his entire empire. If there's one thing she knew about her uncle Barry, it's that he wouldn't just let that slide. If he was ever going to take revenge, Jamie and her friends would be helpless without each other.

The girls were about to head back to the house as Jamie prepared this image of summer happiness to share on her socials.

'Oh, Jamie, are you going to post that photo?' asked Daisy.

'Yeah, I was just about to, why?' Jamie replied, her stomach sinking.

'Do you mind if I just run it by Talia? I know it's annoying but she's asked me to consult with her before posting anything that may not be **DAISY BRAND.** Not sure if a Queen Gnome costume fits with her content strategy—'

'Talia, Talia, Talia, Talia,' said Jenners in a mocking voice.

'I'm sorry!' said Daisy 'But Talia says this is a very important time in my influencing career!'

'Talia doesn't control Jamie; she can post what she likes,' grumbled Jenners.

'It's OK, Jenners,' said Jamie, who cared more about enjoying the last few weeks with her closest friends than anything to do with social media, even though this had been going on all summer and was **REALLY ANNOYING.** 'I hope Talia's cool with it, because it is a really good photo.'

Talia was Daisy's PR manager, who was sort of like another mum but for social media. As you can probably guess, being the heroes who'd saved a festival from a monstrous boyband had shone a spotlight on the girls. Talia would regularly nag Daisy to keep posting photos that would make her **POPULAR** in internet-land.

'Should I get a PR manager?' asked Mel. 'Maybe if I got a PR manager, I wouldn't get my head flushed down the toilet at Bobbinson Comprehensive?' A prospect that had terrified Mel and worried Jamie all summer.

'That's not going to happen, Mel. If it does, I'll run in and go **FULL JENZILLA** on people,' said Jenners, who despite her tough exterior had been secretly terrified about going to Strumptons High School on her own. A secret that only Jamie knew.

'Besides, you and that goose are pretty internet famous now – maybe you'll have fans and stuff?' added Daisy.

The infamous Crudwell 'goose on the loose', who now never seemed to leave Mel's side, had been sitting watching the girls with Buttons, the cutest pug in Crudwell. The animals adorably waddled and bounded over.

'Oh, hey, Mr Goose!' said Mel, wrapping her arms around the thin neck that was now honking angrily in Jamie's direction. Since Mel had found the goose, they'd become a popular TikTok double act as the goose's strange antics lent themselves well to short-form video content.

Jamie was unsure about the goose. She was almost certainly not jealous of Mel and the goose's friendship and definitely not jealous of its internet superstardom. That would be silly, wouldn't it? Too silly for a brain that's about to go into Year 7. She gave Buttons a reassuring snuggle.

The goose then started honking at Henrik, probably because he was loads higher up the food chain. Henrik looked nervous and confused. He removed his fez and placed it over the goose's head, muffling the honks.

'It's the weirdest goose I've ever seen,' said Daisy, 'and we've seen quite a lot of weird creatures recently. No offence, Henrik.'

Suddenly all the girls' phones buzzed at once with the same message.

NOTIFICATION
NICA KONSTANTOPOLOUS
SHOE LAUNCH EVENT in 2 HRS

'I didn't realise this was so soon!' yelled Jenners with some added language that isn't suitable for books. **JAMIE'S HEART SANK.** She thought they'd have more time to play. Being invited to weird parties was probably Jamie's least favourite part of being mildly internet famous, but at least they were all going to this one together.

'I wonder how high the shoes will be launched?' asked Mel excitedly.

'Hopefully SPACE! Apparently, Nica's bandmate got launched into space once. Could be fake news though,' added Jenners.

You'll remember Nica from being the least mean judge on Barry's old show, *The Big Time*. After the girls exposed Barry, *The Big Time* was cancelled and replaced by an even weirder show where celebrities from the past sang in strange, masked costumes. Nica was now a judge on that show, along with . . .

'Is Scott going to be there?' asked Daisy.

Scott was Jamie's favourite member of the girls' favourite band, BNA. Since the events of the World Music Festival, and the restoration of their talents, BNA had rightfully become **MASSIVE.** *If you ever need me, give me a shout in the DMs and we'll be there. We owe you!* was a DM from Scott that Jamie had printed and framed in her room.

'No, BNA are at a palooza tonight. Whatever that is,' said Jamie. 'It would be great to see Nica, though.'

'Maybe she knows where your uncle Barry is?' said Mel, who had been hoping for Barry Bigtime's capture all summer.

44

'Could be a trap? Maybe Barry's got Nica to poison the free snacks or something?' said Jenners.

'Hmm, I don't think she was in on his horrible plans. She always seemed so nice,' said Jamie. 'Plus, Scott works with her on TV and says she's really friendly. I just want to ask her what Barry was REALLY like. Why did he ever do all the mean things he did?'

The girls nodded.

'I also wonder why he needed a garden that was so ridiculously massive?' said Jenners.

'Um, I'm all up for fashionable lateness, guys, but we are still **MILES** away from your house.' Daisy laughed.

'Barry BigGardens!' said Mel, a little too late.

Good point, Daisy. Good joke, Mel,' said Jamie. 'Do you mind carrying us back to the house, Henrik?'

'Yeah, we couldn't possibly be late . . .' yelled Jenners. **'I CAN'T WAIT** to see Nica Konstantopolous's new shoes!' She giggled sarcastically. The girls laughed as Henrik looked confused.

'Jenners is joking, Henrik,' said Jamie, knowing the bear struggled with sarcasm.

'If you ever see us being legitimately excited about Nica Konstantopolous shoes, Henrik, you'll know we're in trouble,' said Jenners to more laughter.

'All aboard,' yelled Henrik as Jenners climbed on to the bear's back. Mel clung on to a leg and, with Daisy and Jamie under each arm, Henrik began the reasonably long journey from the garden to Jamie's home.

Or what would be Jamie's home . . . **FOR NOW.**

CHAPTER 5

Nica Konstantopolous's Shoes

'Got some visitors for you, Mrs McFlair!' chimed Henrik as he strode into the marshmallow room.

Jamie's mum and grandma were lying down in a room that was made **ENTIRELY OF CUSHIONS AND OTHER BOUNCY COMFORTABLE THINGS.** Jamie's uncle Barry used to use it to calm his tantrums. Grandma was relaxing, using Sheamus the pet pig as a pillow. The old lady had spent the morning being annoyed by made-up stories that she saw on Facebook. Today, Jamie's mum, Sarah, was using it to relax after several days of packing up the mansion and dealing with estate surveyor grown-ups. You see, Jamie, her mum and Grandma had come to the joint decision to **SELL THE MANSION.**

Living in the mansion never really sat right with

Jamie, her mum or Grandma. They'd never had much money before and definitely didn't need a house with fifty-six rooms. The mansion never really felt like THEIR home. The ghosts of Uncle Barry were still popping up seven months later. The final straw was discovering a **HIDDEN UNDERGROUND ZOO** full of feral musical animals.

'Thanks, Henrik, love,' Sarah said. 'Oh, while I remember, I'm afraid you'll have to make yourself scarce for a few hours tomorrow. There's people coming to look at the house who want to turn the land back into fun park things for Crudwell.'

'That's exactly what we were hoping for!' Jamie beamed. The family had turned down big offers from people who smelt a little too big-time for their liking. They really wanted the land to go back to the Crudwell community like it had before Barry built the mansion, because they're good eggs like that.

'That sounds wonderful, Mrs M!' said Henrik cheerfully. Sarah loved Henrik; he made her and Jamie feel more safe, but having a talking bear in the house was never going to not be strange for her.

'Anyways, glad you're all safe, dear!' Sarah said.

'Safe? We were only in the garden, Mum,' Jamie replied.

It's important to realise that, after the events of the World Music Festival, worry among parents had increased nationwide by a whopping 423 per cent. Despite government insistence that such a monster-related incident would **NEVER HAPPEN AGAIN,** parents were outraged and concerned about the safety of their children. As they always are. There'd even been a week of school assemblies about how to spot monster defects and to look out for any strange changes in your friends. This led to a boy in Year 6 reporting his classmate to the police for having the beginnings of a moustache, which led to a further assembly on the normal changes that children go through at a certain age.

'Sorry, love, I'm just being silly. Lot on my mind,

you see!' said Sarah wearily.

'Well, stop being silly and start getting ready, Mum,' said Jamie jokingly. 'We need to be at Nica Konstantopolous's new shoe launch in, well, less than two hours.'

'Why don't I give you a lift in my new wheels?' said Grandma, who tried to sit up but sort of rolled over on her side. **'Then you can arrive in STYLE!'**

Sheamus the pig gave a grumbly oink of agreement.

'No, I don't think—' began Jamie's mum.

The girls immediately broke out into cheers of excitement. They'd been waiting to ride in Grandma's new wheels ALL summer. Grandma had upgraded her mobility scooter to a bright white stretch limousine. A stretch limousine is essentially a really long car. Famous people would use it to turn up to special events in the 1990s. Nowadays they're mostly used for end-of-Year-11 proms. In the back there were sofas and a Nintendo Switch, along with delightful refreshments such as Guggleschrumpf, cookies and juice. The girls had been wanting a ride as soon as possible before it started to smell too much like Grandma.

Jamie's mum looked uneasy (and she didn't even know about the time Grandma took Jamie for a ride on a stolen tour bus).

'Do you definitely know how to drive that thing, Mum?' said Sarah.

'Oh, of course! I swear on Reginald Whittaker's grave,' replied Grandma, giving the girls a wink.

*

'Aaaaahhh!'

'Oooohhh Lord!'

'I don't WANNA DIE!'

'SLOW DOWN!'

'WAAAAHH!'

'THIS IS AWESOME!'

'MUM, FOR GOODNESS' SAKE!'

HONK, HONK, HONK!

'It's HERE, Grandma!'

'Mum, SLOW DOWN!'

'No, Grandma, it's here. GRANDMA, STOP!'

'MUMMM!' came the shouts from the limousine.

Grandma power-slid the limo across seven empty car park spaces and lurched to a halt.

In the back, puddles of Guggleschrumpf, cookie crumbs, juice, Joy-Cons and goose feathers were strewn over the fancy upholstery.

'Mum, you **CAN'T** drive like that with the girls in the back, seriously,' said Jamie's mum, unbuckling her seat belt with a trembling hand.

'Oh come on, where's your Christmas spirit?' said Grandma as the evening August sun beamed on to her thinning clumps of grey hair.

Jamie stepped out of the limousine, legs wobbling, followed by Jenners, who bounded out of the car as if she'd just skydived out of a battle bus.

'THAT. WAS. BRILLIANT. Mabez, you're actually a legend.'

Mabel was what everyone else called Jamie's grandma because that was her name. Jenners, however, called her Mabez because they shared a **WEIRD BOND.** Mel was so wobbly she looked like she was going to pass out. Jamie put an arm around her friend as the goose watched on with a cold stare. Troubling. Meanwhile, Daisy, unsurprisingly, was on the phone.

'Hi, Talia – yeah, just got here. Oh no, I'm fine, was **a wild ride,** that's all. So what are the content expectations for this event?'

The group started to make their way out of the car park, apart from Jamie's mum, who was left to buy seven pay-and-display tickets.

'It's about time I took that old girl for a proper spin,' said Grandma to Jamie with a wink and a click of the remote lock. 'Very hard to find parking, though, that's the trouble.'

Tandy's was the **POSHEST** place in Crudwell by miles. It was where you would go for special occasions like winning the lottery. As the girls wobbled to the entrance, they were greeted by a lady who looked like she'd been permanently smiling for all twenty-five years of her existence.

'Hiii, guuuys,' she bleated, lingering

annoyingly on each 'eye' sound. 'It's our resident monster slayers! Our guests of honour! Oh, and the world's favourite goose! And of course superfan Mum! . . . I don't seem to have Grandma on the list.'

'We both know that you're not going to leave an old lady out in the cold!' said the hot and sweaty Grandma as she **BARGED PAST THE LADY** into the event.

The pulsing Nica Konstantopolous tunes swept over the girls as they shuffled through the door. The decorations looked expensive and mostly pointless. Plus, the room was filled with more Nica cardboard cut-outs than there were actual guests at the event. Dotted around was also the odd shoe. Jamie didn't want to waste time. She wanted to find Nica before things got too busy.

Jamie soon got bored being confused by the Nica cardboard cut-outs and the **GIANT 3D VIRTUAL** Nica that was dancing through a city. She decided to ask a grown-up where she was.

'Excuse me, do you know where Nica is?' Jamie

asked the most stable-looking person she could find.

'Nica isn't here right now,' the older lady said apologetically.

'Well, when is she arriving?' said Jamie, confused at why Nica would be late to her own shoe launch.

'Unfortunately, she isn't going to be here tonight at all,' said the lady as Jamie's jaw dropped.

'But . . . why, after she's made all of these shoes?' asked Jamie.

'Well . . . Nica didn't actually physically make the shoes as such—'

'OK, well, after she spent all her time designing them—'

'Well . . . Nica didn't actually design the shoes herself—'

'Well, if she didn't make or design them, **what did she do?'**

'Let's get you girls some free juice!' said the exasperated lady.

Jenners, Daisy, Mel and Grandma were already at

the refreshments table. Jenners's plate was stacked high with a variety of **POSH FOODS ON STICKS.** Daisy stood out the least at the posh event because her fashion sense was from the land of cool people. Even some of the adults there couldn't pull off a leather jacket and velvet beret like Daisy. She had light brown skin, blonde hair and could start a conversation with anyone. Jenners, on the other hand, was not from posh fashion land. Instead, she had her long brown hair scraped back tightly and tied in a bun. She had broader shoulders than the other girls and wore her favourite football shirt because **THAT'S WHAT SHE WANTED TO WEAR.** Besides, she was taller than most of the boys in her class, who would usually think twice about making fun of her. Mel had pale skin and wore a sun hat indoors because she was Mel. Jamie's flame-red hair completed the troupe.

'What's wrong, Jamie?' asked Mel, who had good sadness-detection skills.

'This is pointless. Nica's not even here!?' said Jamie, who also felt guilty dragging her mum here when she was so busy and stressed about the house.

'Also, they're not actually launching the shoes anywhere. They're just coming out in the shops. **How lame is that?'** said Jenners, angrily chomping on a meat lolly. 'Apparently, if we want to see any shoes being actually launched then we have to throw them ourselves.'

'Where's Daisy?' asked Jamie.

'She's just getting a selfie with all the shoes,' added Jenners. 'May as well make the most of the food, though. We never get to go to Tandy's, because Mum got barred for the **TABLE-SLAMMING INCIDENT**. Surprised they let me in, to be honest.'

Jamie was annoyed about the lack of Nica, but was determined to make the most of the remaining summer friend-time, so started scanning the room for crumbs of excitement while also spilling crumbs of a cracker that had just finished delivering posh cheese into her gob.

'If you think about it, a cracker is a bit like a plate for cheese that you can eat,' said Mel, who actually

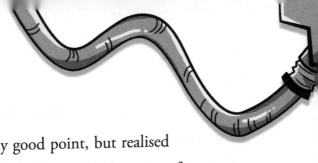

made a really good point, but realised Jamie had already left in the direction of some glitzy merchandise stalls in the corner of the room. She fed the rest of her cracker to the goose and scampered after her pals.

Jamie had low expectations for the first merch stall, although to be fair, the man in charge did seem excited.

'The name's William Clarkson, but everyone calls me **Billy,**' the man announced. He seemed friendly enough but had a very faint whiff of stranger danger. Jamie was on her guard. Even the goose, who was trailing along behind Mel, **NARROWED ITS EYES.**

Billy Clarkson, a name that should ring a suspicious bell from the first book, had been partying every day since 1976. For a man well into his sixties, his skin was immaculate but his eyes were tired.

'I was very good friends with Nica Konstantopolous. Do you remember her from *The Big Time*?'

'Obviously we do,' said Jenners while chomping on

a chicken-and-herb skewer. **'Why else would we be here?'**

'Do you know where she is?' asked Jamie. 'I really want to speak to her.'

'I have something far more interesting to tell you about,' said Clarkson. He opened his shoulder bag and pulled out a booklet entitled **RUBBSLINGS SCHOOL FOR CREATORS AND INFLUENCERS.**

'As fans of Nica, you'll know she has a passion for

upcoming talent, hence her involvement in *The Big Time*,' Billy went on.

At least she used to actually show up to The Big Time, thought Jamie.

'Well, she has now put her **stamp of approval** on the Rubbslings School for Creators and Influencers. It's a school that will guarantee its students millions of followers before graduation. You will learn how to make the coolest videos and the funniest TikToks! Our island educational paradise is also the **SAFEST** school in the whole world! With the latest anti-monster safety technology. Not that we'd need it with the famous Jamie McFlair around . . .' Billy said, waving his arms in a way that created **STRONG MYSTIQUE.**

Jamie looked at the booklet sceptically. *An internet school?* Sounded stupid and made-up. Why were people so **OBSESSED** with followers? She was far more worried about spending the last days of summer with her in-real-life friends. However, if the school was monster-proof, it must be Barry-Bigtime-proof. *Wherever he may be . . .* Her thoughts were interrupted as Daisy arrived, mid vlog.

'So, guys, I've just had this Nica Konstantopolous merch **gifted to me.** The hat is actually really good material, the fidget spinner would be great if it was three years ago aaand I'm gonna do some of her yoga content for you soon!' said Daisy into her phone.

'You got all of that stuff for free?' asked Jamie.

Daisy held up a hand for quiet. 'Yeah, wait, sorry, Jamie, let me just post this so Talia is happy.'

'I want free stuff,' said Jenners.

'You're literally chewing on your fourth free chocolate strawberry,' said Jamie, frowning at Daisy's raised hand.

'Fair,' replied Jenners, and wandered off.

'Excuse me! Girls! Let me give you a brochure,' hollered Billy Clarkson, who was slightly annoyed that his mystique-creating skills were being underappreciated. 'The places are very exclusive, but I imagine you four would stand a good chance,' he said, thrusting booklets made of glossy, non-recycled paper at them.

'No thank you,' said Jamie politely. 'Come on, let's go, we can play more Flower Samurais before it gets dark!'

'Creator school! Cool!' said Daisy, perking up as she grabbed the four brochures, before spotting Jamie's disgruntled face and stuffing them in her bag. Jamie was about to object when a **£800 BEJEWELLED SANDAL** flew past her head. She spun round to spot two rogue, giggling shoe-launchers.

'WE HAVE LIFT-OFF,' yelled Jenners as another shoe took to the sky.

'**ONE SMALL STEP FOR SHOES, ONE GIANT LEAP FOR . . . SHOES,**' yelled Grandma as she threw a stiletto like a discus.

'I think your grandma is about to get us **kicked out,** Jamie,' said Daisy.

Daisy was correct as, soon enough, they were all squashed in the back of a taxi. (Grandma had sloshed

down too many free wines to be able to drive the limousine home.)

Jenners helped Sarah ease a **STUMBLY** Grandma up the gravelly path to Jamie's house. Henrik greeted them at the door.

'You're back early!' the bear said cheerily.

'Grandma got us kicked out.' Jamie giggled.

'Not again!' Henrik laughed.

'You promised you'd get your act together before Ethel's cruise, Mum,' said an exasperated Sarah. 'You behave like that on board and they'll throw you in the sea.'

'If they throw me in the sea . . . **I'll swim home,**' slurred Grandma, eyes askew.

'Need a lift, Jamie?' asked Henrik, keen to break the tension.

Jamie nodded.

The girls climbed aboard Henrik as he took them to the **MARSHMALLOW ROOM,** which had become the designated sleepover zone.

It was pretty clear that another game of Flower

Samurais of Death was out of the question once all four girls and even Buttons had become sleeping-bag burritos, wrapped up tightly and ready to watch *Animals with Attitude*, a film they had all seen about eleven times before and **KNEW EVERY WORD TO.** It wasn't long before Jenners had cracked out her Sassy Monkey impression and all four of them were struggling to breathe from laughing so much.

'Stopppp!' said Mel, crying full tears of laughter and trying to get valuable oxygen into her lungs. 'I'm gonna throw up.' This sent Daisy into an absolute fit of giggles, confusing Buttons, who left the room to the safety of Jamie's mum's bed.

As the girls promised each other that they 'were just resting their eyes' and one by one fell asleep, Jamie lay awake. Her brain was always the one that had the most questions. **AFTER THE SUMMER, WOULD NIGHTS LIKE THIS STILL BE A THING?** Would anyone at her next school even know what *Animals With Attitude* was? Would people make fun of Mel because she wore clothes that weren't cool, and Jenners because she was Jenners? Would Daisy get so big on social media that she wouldn't want to hang out any more? Jamie felt like she wanted to **PROTECT HER FRIENDS.** She took a deep breath, let out a big sigh and tried to stop thinking unhelpful things.

Jamie woke up late the next morning to find the other girls weren't there. The marshmallow room looked like a bigger marshmallow had hit it; there were snacks, rubbish and clothes everywhere.

Jamie rubbed her eyes and accidentally stood on a pile of cheese puffs, which **CRUNCHED** between her toes. As she looked down, she spotted a Rubbslings brochure on the floor and picked it up.

Jamie joined the girls in the kitchen. She helped herself to some Henrik pancakes and placed the brochure on the table.

'What do we think about this?' she asked the others. 'A school for creators where you get followers? Is this a thing?' Jamie asked the group.

Mel and Jenners leant in to have a look, while Daisy focused on getting a really good pancake picture for Instagram.

'I guess it's for influencers. **Influencers always get cool stuff.** So why not have a cool school?' said Jenners.

'I'm not sure I'm cool enough for cool school . . .' said Mel glumly. 'Are even the lessons cool?'

'Well, it says here that instead of normal schoolwork, they teach you how to make really clever videos and stuff like that,' said Jamie.

'It also says it welcomes influencer pets! You could take the goose with you!' said Jenners as **MEL'S FACE BRIGHTENED.**

'None of it looks proper, though,' said Jamie. 'Are we going to get A levels in . . . YouTube drama? Crypto . . . something or other?'

'To be fair, Lady Day makes more money with a single Instagram post than some people make ever,' said

Jenners. 'Plus, A levels, Jamie? They're like a million years away.'

'Fair point,' said Jamie, nodding in agreement. 'What do you think, Daisy?'

Daisy didn't reply. She looked annoyed as she repeatedly took pancake pictures.

'Daisy?' Jamie asked again, a little louder.

'Sorry, I'm trying to post this, but yes, Talia thought I should apply to the school so I have sent the form already.'

'Oh . . .' said Jamie, a little taken aback. 'Were you going to tell us that?'

'Yeah, **obviously!** Definitely send the form as well, it only takes two minutes! We could all go and you get a new phone and laptop when you arrive, the whole thing is on an island, it sounds **amazing!'** Daisy replied.

Mel, who was starting to not feel anxious for the first time this summer, piped up. 'And if it means we stay together **AND** I can take the goose, then I think this may cure my stress rash.'

Jamie flicked through the brochure some more. A creator school sounded **WEIRD** – she had never been fussed about getting followers – but if it meant her friends could all stay together, surely that was a good thing. She thought back to the mornings she'd spent dreaming about being a YouTuber so she could move her family into a nicer house. She thought about the BNAspace community she'd created two years ago, and the TikToks she'd made to classic BNA songs. Plus lessons in VR did sound **QUITE COOL** . . . And if it was on a monster-proof island, they would be safe from Uncle Barry there.

Jamie's idea-seed started to blossom and as the sapling of thought started growing, the school started to seem a lot less stupid, and a lot less made-up, and a lot more awesome and a lot more essential. Jamie's tummy got more **EXCITED** as the answers to every problem and fear she'd had over the summer seemed to lie inside this booklet.

'We should go,' she said confidently to the others.

'What about our other school places, though? I

don't think my mum is just gonna let me go to internet school. She sent my brother off to a boarding school after everything that happened last summer . . .' Mel said nervously.

'MUM!' yelled Jamie. 'Can the girls stay again tonight?'

'If it's all right with their parents, it's all right with me!' Sarah shouted back from the hallway.

'Tonight, we make a plan,' said Jamie.

CHAPTER 6
BIGTIME WASN'T BUILT IN A DAY

Barry was feeling **GRUBULOUS,** which is a word which we've made up to describe someone who is fabulous but in an evil way.

'SO! Are we all clear on the next stages of Operation Rubbslings?' Barry beamed, arms wide, face unsettling.

Slottapuss and Flobster looked at each other. They had been involved in some weird Barry Bigtime schemes in the past. They'd been Barry's burger chefs, there was the whole Barryland fiasco and of course many years of questionable boyband generation. This plan was certainly the most . . . **AMBITIOUS.**

Slottapuss looked at the Rubbslings School for Creators and Influencers brochure. It looked like garbage, therefore tasty, and he didn't understand many of the words. He also looked around the freshly built 'classroom' that he and Flobster were sitting in. He couldn't be sure but he was certain human classrooms were meant to have chairs instead of a **BALL PIT,** although this *was* comfortable and colourful.

Slottapuss glanced at Flobster, who after six months of intense school-construction assistance was lying in the arms of a fourteen-foot-tall stuffed gorilla. The gorilla also didn't look like a usual classroom item. In fact, it also looked quite grubulous. Slottapuss's little rat eyes then moved to the smartboard displaying Barry's plan, which was written in the completely **UNACCEPTABLE** Jokerman font.

'OK, so Step 1: Build a massive school that internet-famous people will find fun. We've definitely done that,' said Slottapuss, holding up some colourful balls. 'Step 2a: Get internet-famous people to enrol in the school to get even more internet-famous . . . Have we done that?' said Slottapuss, hoping that wasn't his job and he'd just forgotten . . .

'Yes, our old friend Billy Clarkson is on the case and has enlisted some of the most influential . . . uhm . . . influencers to our school, on the promise that they will become even more . . . uhm . . . influential . . . ous,' said Barry, who was also making up words today.

Slottapuss nodded.

'He also has another very special part of his mission, which I need him to knuckle down on or **I'll knuckle his skull in,**' spat Barry.

'Is that Step 2b: Jamie McFlair and her friends enrol in the school so we can extract . . . vengeful . . . rev . . . does that say "revenge"?' **FLOBSTER SQUINTED.**

'Yes, and there's no word of her planned arrival yet and that is making me vexed,' snarled Barry.

'Step 3,' said Slottapuss, keen to move on. 'Get some teachers . . . This bit seems important for a school,' said the rat beast, who for one second wondered what one of the ball pit balls would taste like.

'Billy Clarkson knows some washed-up YouTubers

of the past. He's dealing with that,' said Barry.

'Step 4,' said Slottapuss. 'Influencer students gain a total of one billion followers while at the school, at which point we commence the **ULTIMATE BRAIN HACK** . . . OK, I think we could do with going through this bit again . . .' said Slottapuss, acknowledging the absurdness of one of the most outrageous sentences of all time.

Barry flounced. 'How many more times, you pea-brained abomination of musical science! It's simple. We gather all of the most famous influencers at the school. We then build up their followings until they have **one billion combined followers** . . .'

'And then we give them social media gummy bears that actually make them fall asleep and then we steal their talents?' said Flobster.

Barry gritted his teeth.

'We already did that plan!' yelled Barry. 'Slottapuss, throw five coloured balls at Flobster immediately.'

'Yes, boss. Sorry, Flob,' said Slottapuss.

'Right, where was I?' continued Barry over the

sound of plastic bouncing on shellfish. 'Oh yes. Once all our influencer students have a combined one billion followers, the Ultimate Brain Hack will bring them under our control. Then we shall use them to start restoring the good name of Barry Bigtime. Finally, Step 5, and arguably the most important—'

Proudy from Baezone, one of Barry's original boyband creations, burst through a door wearing nothing but a tribal loincloth for reasons we **PROMISE** we'll explain later. 'Sorry, lads,' said Proudy. 'Materials for Mr Bigtime's top-secret island hideout are about to arrive.'

'We'll come back to this later,' yelled Barry.

The bizarre little foursome left the classroom, into an unfinished corridor that gave intense prison vibes, then out into the blustery island breeze. Bustling construction was still taking place. Taking care of most of the heavy lifting were Barry's old boyband creations, who had joined him as his own personal influencers back in Chapter 34 of the last book.

Up from the reasonably grey skies, a bouquet of colourful hot air balloons were beginning to descend on to the island. Waving from the basket with his shovel-like hands was Barry's old chum and balloon emporium kingpin, **BRUCE BURRELL.**

You may think that delivering materials for a top-secret scheme by hot air balloon would be terribly impractical but Bruce had been discreetly delivering **NEFARIOUS ITEMS** by balloon since 1995.

One of the balloons also seemed to be carrying an entire castle. It reminded Slottapuss of a film he once saw where a house was tied up to balloons and went up in the sky, but the name of the film escaped him.

Flobster, who was on balloon-direction duties for the second book in a row, shouted up to Bruce, 'Left a bit, down, yes, almost there!'

'Blimmin' 'eck,' said Bruce as he looked around the thriving building site. 'Things are really starting to take shape.'

'It's getting there!' sighed Flobster, who was

exhausted and still had several balloons to land.

Flobster, while being chief balloon director, also had the rather dull job of dealing with all the admin that goes along with an evil plan. Of which there was **PLENTY.** He looked at his phone calendar. Selling diamonds, negotiating with the building contractors, paying off the educational authorities, risk assessments, even down to making sure there were Rubbslings-branded pens in the classrooms. You don't normally hear about that side of an **EVIL SCHEME,** mainly because it is terribly tedious. Nobody wants to see a villain doing an invoice. Really kills the mystique. Oh, you'd rather know more about the castle that arrived by balloon? Perfectly understandable – our apologies.

The castle was an unused structure for Barry's failed theme park experiment called Barryland. The park had run out of money before it even managed to open, but with building times for the Rubbslings School running behind schedule, Barry had decided to recycle bits of the failed **THEME PARK** around the school. The castle was to be Barry's hideout quarters.

This was the most important part of the school for Barry – his presence must be kept a **SECRET,** as he was still wanted by Detective Lansdown.

'Excuse me one second, Bruce,' said Flobster, who had to shout some voice commands at his phone (as his under-the-sea claws made touch screens impossible).

'Siri, message Proudy from Baezone. "Don't forget you've got a Zoom meeting with the new teachers later. Remember Barry Bigtime is a secret. Ask someone to move new secret machine into castle. Kiss."'

Because Flobster was a **TERRIFYING LOBSTER MONSTER,** Proudy dealt with a lot of the face-to-face meetings, which made Proudy happy because he was helping but sad because nobody ever recognised who he was.

'Brucey!' said Barry, patting his long-time friend on the head like a good pup. 'Your support, discretion and loyalty during these testing times is always very appreciated! Slotty, show this man our

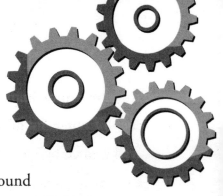

gratitude by greasing his palm with trinkets!' Barry said pompously.

Slottapuss rummaged around in his jacket and brandished **A DIAMOND-ENCRUSTED SPATULA** and a Rubbslings School-branded pen and popped them in Bruce's outstretched man-hand.

'It's a pleasure, Mr Bigtime,' said Bruce, examining the spatula and wondering if he would use it to make or buy food.

'SLOTTY!' hollered Barry for the forty-second time that day.

'I'm standing right here,' said Slottapuss, holding his ringing ears.

'Prepare the castle! There we shalt go through Point 5 of Phase 2 of Operation Rubbslings.' The prospect of the castle was accidentally making Barry talk like a king.

'Point 5?' asked Slottapuss, who could only remember up to the Ultimate Brain Hack bit. 'What was that one again?'

'Make Jamie McFlair pay,' said Barry with a grubulous grin.

CHAPTER 7

MAKING A POWERFUL POINT

'Do you think we should add some more colours on the slides, maybe a few more cool fade-out transitions or maybe a star wipe?' asked Mel in panicky Mel mode, which was also **NORMAL MEL MODE,** as she looked at the time on her phone.

'You can but quickly! And only colours that parents will like, maybe a quite boring lilac or off-white cream, not bright colours that make it look **too fun,**' Jamie instructed as she finished tying her flame-red hair into a more professional grown-up bun.

Last night's sleepover will not go down in the history books of 'Funnest Sleepovers Ever', mainly because the girls spent the majority of the night working on a slide show. Slide shows (which have a fun rating of -10) are sometimes necessary for parents to understand plans, and in this case the objective was to convince their parents that Rubbslings School was a **'GOOD CHOICE FOR THEIR FUTURE'.** Other highlights of the sleepover did, however, include Jenners performing a wrestling suplex with Daisy on the sofa and Mel almost deleting the entire slide show during a dance-off with Grandma's pet pig, Sheamus. We just thought you should know that it wasn't all sensible.

The girls had chosen the Brilliant Hall for the presentation, which had a stage and projector and was previously used for Barry's far more elaborate **CELEBRITY PARTIES** of nonsense. It could fit about a hundred people but today the chairs were filled with just Sarah, her boyfriend Dominic, Jenners's mum, Mel's mum and Daisy's mum, who weren't there for a party, but had all come to pick up their daughters from the sleepover. Oh, and also Buttons, who was chewing on a rubber chicken and seemed to be having a nice, squeaky time.

Jamie huddled the girls behind the stage. 'OK, we

all know our roles, right? Daisy, you head out with the tray of tea, make them feel welcome, give them a bit of chit-chat, you're good at that.'

Daisy nodded and got to work. She wandered down the stage steps towards the parents. 'Usual milk and five sugars, is it, Mrs Tregwell?' she asked.

Jamie continued, 'I'll start the presentation, up until the bit about being able to FaceTime us every day. Then, Jenners, you step in.'

'**Got it,**' said Jenners, who now firmly had her game face on.

'And Mel, you've got the most important job of all: press right on the keyboard to change the slides and try to make sure nothing goes wrong. You'll know when because I'll say, "Next slide, please."'

Mel, who already looked **OVERLY STRESSED** with the responsibility, managed a nod.

'And we're live in five . . . four . . . three . . . two . . .' Jamie walked out on to the gigantic Brilliant Hall stage and looked at the parents. 'Welcome to our presentation to show you why we think the four of us going to Rubbslings School for Creators and Influencers is a good decision for our future,' she said **CONFIDENTLY.**

The next ten minutes was a **WHIRLWIND** of trying to explain the internet, how being a YouTuber is actually a **REAL JOB** and persuading grown-ups that generating millions of views might be more useful than knowing how sedimentary rocks are formed. The girls had included every type of graph to make it really hit home and images of old-school YouTuber StompyDog's four-million-dollar mansion, which he bought with cash from his unboxing videos. (However, they did leave out the bit where StompyDog lost all his money buying online dog-themed coins.)

Once her bit was over, Jamie breathed a sigh of relief, as did Mel, who had really nailed changing the slides on time.

'Now I'd like to hand over to my friend and colleague, Jennifer Tregwell.'

'Thank you, Jamie McFlair, for that really **in-depth explanation of the internet.** I'd like to just borrow five minutes more of your time to show you what career opportunities Rubbslings School for Creators and Influencers can offer us,' said Jenners, using almost entirely words that she'd heard parents say at parents' evenings.

Jenners confidently powered through jobs such as gamer, fashion influencer, lifestyle Instagrammer and **SOCIAL MEDIA MANAGER** before thanking everyone for their time and gathering the rest of the girls back on stage.

'And the brochure says, "If parents wish to find out more, then they are welcome to join a Rubbslings School representative for an **all-expenses-paid** luncheon at a restaurant of your choice on the weekend of your choice",' finished Jamie.

There was a round of applause from the parents and rightly so because, truth be told, the girls had smashed it out of the park.

Mel's mum, who was definitely where Mel got her panic from, popped up her hand with a worried expression. 'Has this school sufficiently prepared for students with any . . . monster defects? **How safe is it?'**

'I'll take this one,' said Jenners, stepping up.

'Rubbslings has the latest in monster-neutralising technology. If a monster shows, it's going to get fully dealt with. Probably safer than normal school. Plus, every student has to complete a How to Stay Safe Online test before they go.'

'Can you further your wrestling career?' asked Jenners's mum, Geraldine, who people either called Ger, or by her wrestling name, **GERCULES.** (As in Hercules. But Ger . . . You get the point.)

'Not now, Mum,' said Jenners, who, despite being at a wrestling level way above her age bracket, wasn't convinced she wanted to follow in Gercules's footsteps as five-time British women's heavyweight champion.

'Girls, it was a brilliant presentation, I can see why you all would be great in front of the camera,' said Sarah. 'And Mel, those transitions, really something.'

Mel smiled. She knew that **STAR WIPE** had been the right decision.

'But it's just not a sensible decision for your future,' she continued, delivering a slice of reality pie. I know you all want to **stay together** but you can't let that sway your choice. Plus, it's a boarding school, it's miles away and you already have your school places arranged. We'll talk about it, Jamie, but let these girls get back to their mothers so they can enjoy some of their weekends. And we've got more people coming round to look at the house any minute, so I need you all out of my hair.'

The girls instantly felt **GLUM** in the way that you do when parents say **'WE'LL TALK ABOUT IT',** which usually means 'no'.

'Can't you just go and meet the Rubbslings School person for the free luncheon at least?' said Jamie.

The parents looked unsure.

'It's free food!' said Jenners. 'You all go and have weekend pub dinners anyway. Why not have a free one? You can choose anywhere! You could even go to one of the posh places that you always say are too expensive!'

'I'm not having a lunch with some stranger I don't know,' said Gercules.

'You went for dinner with that football scout for Birchester City. You didn't know him,' said Jenners accusingly.

'Different,' grumbled Gercules.

'And you went for dinner with the headmaster of that school that I don't even want to go to!' said Jamie to her mum.

'Yeah, but that was **very different,**' said Sarah.

'Yeah, and you let that man take my teeth out, and you didn't know him!' said Mel.

'That was a dentist!' said Mel's mum.

'Still didn't know him, though, did you?' said Mel, arms folded.

'Don't you love us?' said Daisy, who always knew the exact things to say to get people to do what she wanted.

'What do you think, Chandice?' asked Gercules.

Chandice, who was Daisy's mum, had two moods. Super mad or super chill. Luckily for Daisy, this was an issue that Chandice was super chill about. 'Daisy's PR manager said it would be a good thing,' she said with a shrug.

'Well . . . I suppose there's no harm in going for lunch . . .' replied Sarah.

'Yessss,' said the girls in unison.

'But that isn't a yes to the school, Jamie,' said Sarah.

The girls nodded. It wasn't the best scenario but the PowerPoint felt like a victory nonetheless.

CHAPTER 8

BARRY BIGTIME'S
ULTIMATE BRAIN HACK

The robbery took place during Gregorius Megacleese's sixtieth birthday celebrations. The thieves not only stole rare, diamond-encrusted collectibles but also the cremated remains of Gregorius's late grandfather. The perpetrators are unknown and still at large.

Barry switched apps and messaged Flobster.

Can we get some troll bots to denounce this diamond robbery story as fake news please? You putrid crustacean abomination! Xx

Barry hadn't felt this **BARRYLICIOUS** for a long time. He was one shark-feeding away from being entirely back to his old self. He was sitting in his new office, perched in the top tower of the **BARRYLAND CASTLE.** A good portion of his diamond haul had been spent on making his office feel sufficiently big-time. Barry sat on a throne made of a stuffed polar bear that had been dyed pink and looked on to a 72-inch 8K flat-screen TV. There was a Jacuzzi, **OBVIOUSLY,** and floor tiles that would change colour when you stepped on them. Long screens lined the walls showing a carousel of Barry's finest moments. **WHAT NONSENSE.**

In the corner of the room was a sculpture of Barry with a wide-open, gaping mouth. Barry dived through the mouth, which led to a twisting, twirling slide. **'Wheeeeee!'** said Barry.

Barry rolled out of the slide landing zone and struggled to his feet. He skipped through the corridors of the Barry Castle that were lined with papier-mâché Barry statues, lovingly made by the boyband creations who had joined him on the island. Barry pulled out his phone and messaged Slottapuss.

SLOTTUMS, GET RID OF THESE HORRID STATUES OF GOO PAPER NOW. THEY ARE CAUSING ME GREAT SADNESS. ORDER PLATINUM REPLACEMENTS. x

Waiting by a pair of grandiose doors were Flobster and Slottapuss, anxiously waiting to hear how Steps 4 and 5 were going to work in Barry's plan.

'Got your message, boss,' said Slottapuss, who had watched Barry type it out from the end of the corridor.

'We can't hang around,' snapped Barry. 'Once we've got you two **CHUCKLEHEADS** up to speed on the new machine, I need to meet a new top-secret special accomplice, so there will be harsh penalties for particularly **STUPID** questions.'

Barry placed his palm on to the **RESTRICTED ACCESS** reader, and the fancy doors slid open. Slottapuss and Flobster's mouths fell open. The room was crammed with many of the **RICKETY AND DANGEROUS** rides from the abandoned Barryland theme park. All of which had failed some sort of health and safety test.

'Here it is, my vile friends!' said Barry. He strutted to a podium that housed a console of complicated buttons and touch screens. **'Barry Bigtime's Ultimate Brain Hack!'** He outstretched his arms and gave a toothy grin.

Flobster and Slottapuss looked around. Raised ten feet in the air was a rollercoaster car. We probably don't even need to tell you that Barry's face was **EMBLAZONED** on the front. Mainly because it's on the cover of the book. Sitting in the car was Fabian from the old boyband The Fenton Dogz. He was wearing a crown of wires and cheerfully waving.

Slottapuss picked his nose and sprinkled the crumbs on the ground. 'Boss, this is all **VERY** cool and a bit messed up, but isn't this supposed to be . . . simpler than the Boyband Generator? Mobile, easy to use anywhere, not limited to having to drag poor schmucks into a weird . . . I don't even know what you'd call this.'

If you're interested in what we'd call this, we'd go for 'stress carnival'.

'It is mobile, Slotty! The Ultimate Brain Hack headgear is controlled remotely and is easily replicable! And the console is essentially just a **massive iPad,**' said Barry, detaching the console from the podium and wafting it at his minions. 'We could have a hundred students wear the Brain Hack headgear in the main school assembly hall and we could gain control of their brains from this very room, the beach or Timbuktu if we fancied,' shouted Barry impatiently.

'So what's all this mad stuff for again?' asked Flobster, gesturing to the ramshackle rollercoaster, teacup ride and makeshift coconut shy.

'I'M BARRY BIGTIME!' yelled Barry. 'Without these fantastic attractions we'd just have some headgear and a big iPad. That's not fun, interesting or fabulous, is it?'

Flobster agreed, keen to avoid the aforementioned harsh penalties.

'But how exactly does this Brain Hack work?' asked Slottapuss, who picked his nose again but this time flicked.

'*Ultimate* Brain Hack, Slotty,' corrected Barry as Slottapuss **GULPED.** 'Well, do you understand second-generation quantum neurological synthesis?'

There were two shakes of the head.

'And do you understand data mining, metabrain and physical brain integration mechanics?'

MORE CONFUSED SHAKES.

'Well then, stop asking stupid questions. All you need to know is this: the headgear hacks the brain, which is then controlled by the console. Once we get our students to a combined one **billion** followers, we shall strike. With these influencers at our control, we'll use them to convince the world that they were wrong about Barry Bigtime, and restore me to my **fame and fortune.**'

'Very 1950s horror movie, boss, love it. But . . . how?' asked Flobster, fighting the urge to grab an interesting-looking red mallet.

'We get the biggest influencers in the world to start clearing my name. #BarryIs Innocent. #BarryBigTime Conspiracy, et cetera. They'll swing public opinion back in my favour. We then use them to push **BIGTIME PRODUCTS,** bring back *The Big Time* show and then who knows what next . . . Barry for prime minister? No . . . I'm joking . . .'

Slottapuss and Flobster didn't think Barry was joking. The **MAGNITUDE** of what Barry had created was starting to hit home. Barry would have control over the world's most influential brains and nobody would be any the wiser. There really would be no limit to the power this machine could bring to its owner.

'All I need to do to get things started is this . . .' Barry picked up a large red mallet. He swung it and **SMASHED** a button that looked a lot like Jamie McFlair's face, which sent a little wooden peg hurtling towards a bell that made a loud **DING!** 'And here we go!' said Barry as the Ultimate Brain Hack fizzed and the rollercoaster car began to move.

With a buzz and a jolt, the car shuddered forward. Then with a **WHOOSH** it plunged down the track and disappeared into the mouth of a large and disturbing replica of Barry Bigtime. The figure of Barry was sprawled out on his front, eyes mechanically rotating. Everybody's eyes followed the track and once it had travelled into the Barrymouth, the car emerged from a tunnel exit, which the Barry figure kept hidden between its buttocks, with a **PLOP AND A BURST OF CONFETTI.**

'Ultimate Brain Hack 50 per cent complete!' squealed Barry excitedly while using the mallet as a dancing cane. The car followed the track, which slotted into a gap on the rickety old teacup ride, which sprang into life. The teacups spun at a speed much faster than would be deemed either safe or enjoyable at a standard fairground. 'Ultimate Brain Hack 75 per cent complete!' yelped Barry, who was now flossing with the mallet.

After a long spin, the car carrying Fabian, who was dizzy from the spinning and befuddled from the Brain Hacking, travelled along a final piece of track, where he was promptly **GUNGED.**

'All done!' chimed Barry cheerfully.

Fabian stepped out of the gooey car and stumbled over to Slottapuss, Flobster and Barry.

'Now, the subject should be unnoticeably different and completely unaware that we can control his brain!' said Barry.

'Won't they wonder why they are slimy, dizzy and full of rollercoaster fun times?' asked Flobster.

'THEY WON'T ALL NEED TO GO ON THE ROLLERCOASTER, FLOBSTACLE. THIS IS JUST TO MAKE THE EARLY EXPERIMENTS FABULOUS!' yelled Barry.

'Anyway, the only way we can control the subject is with this ... the **Console of Ultimate Command!**' said Barry in a **MYSTERIOUS** voice. He picked up the console again and began to tap.

'Now, prepare to be stunned as I drop this thought into the subject's brain ...'

'*Por que sou um menino em um circo? Quem é você?*' said Fabian, wide-eyed, scared and gungy.

'Uh ... I don't remember Fabian being Portuguese

before . . .' said Slottapuss.

Fabian then got on all fours and started barking like he was an actual dog.

'Are you making him be a dog, boss?' asked Flobster sceptically.

'Ah, this blasted thing!' said Barry, slamming a fist on to the console.

'Has the Ultimate Brain Hack worked at all yet?' asked Slottapuss.

'Not . . . perfectly,' said Barry, getting out his phone. 'Proudy, we've had another mishap. Could someone collect the test subject and take him to the boyband tribe camp for quarantine, please. Remember the rule: any sign of monster-fied defects, then straight to the makeshift **CANCELLATION POOL** at the bottom of the cliffs.' Fabian gave a Portuguese bark of fear.

Barry stormed out. His eyes scanned the area for things to smash. *Three weeks till opening day . . . Is that enough time to get this blasted machine to work? It will definitely work . . . It just needs some perfections to the formula . . .*

Barry's phone began to buzz. He looked at the caller ID: **TOP-SECRET NEW ACCOMPLICE.** Very subtle.

'Hello . . . Yes, yes, I was expecting your call . . . William Clarkson has explained the plan? . . . Yes, your job will be to bring Jamie McFlair to me . . . Yes, of course secrecy is the key; the plan is bigger than Jamie McFlair . . . but she does have a tendency to foil plans so don't hang around . . . Yes, yes, the financial rewards will be significant . . . She'll never see you coming . . . Yes . . . Aquatic Experience, Sheringham Harbour, 4 September. See you soon.'

Click.

CHAPTER 9
THE CARVERY IN CYBERSPACE

By the time Saturday rolled around, there had been much talk of the **FREE LUNCH.** Dominic had been unusually mysterious about where he'd chosen for their free grub. 'I think you'll like it,' was all he would give away on the journey there.

Dominic pulled up into the gravelly car park of the Monty Cod with a smile on his face.

'Dominic!? Out of all the places you could've chosen, this is the pub we go to every weekend anyway!' said Sarah, annoyed she'd missed out on some potentially premium grub.

'But we like this place!' said Dominic as they wandered in to meet the others.

Billy Clarkson was dressed extremely fabulously in an **ELECTRIC-PINK SUIT,** with a frilled white shirt and a hat that would've been suitable for a royal wedding.

'You must be Sarah! Lovely, darling, just lovely to meet you!' he said, embracing her as if she was a long-lost twin. 'And Dominic, of course! My, what a handsome chap – what **ravishing sideburns** you have.'

Dominic could only stutter a garbled 'Than . . . k . . . y . . . ou' because no one had complimented his sideburns before.

Billy turned to the rest of the table, where Gercules, Mel's mum, and Chandice sat scanning the menus.

'Order whatever your heart desires! If you want three courses, have four! If one drink won't quench your thirst, have seven! It is all on me, don't you worry about a thing!' said Billy, performing a spin and pausing for applause, which never quite arrived.

Instead, the parents made a series of 'ooh' and 'well go on then' sorts of noises as they gladly accepted Billy's offer and went for the full works premium pub grub.

'. . . and a couple of bottles of your finest wine of the red flavour, please,' added Billy in the direction of the **BEFUDDLED WAITER.** 'Now then, while we wait for our delicious food, I have a little something to show you.'

Billy handed Dominic, Sarah, Chandice, Gercules and Mel's mum a **VR HEADSET** each. 'Now I totally understand. This internet school you've been chatting about with your daughters, it all sounds a little bit **mumbo-jumbo technology-speak,** all a little far-fetched. I get it, I do, but pop this on over your head – we're about to go on a little journey.'

The parents briefly struggled with their headsets, saying things like 'Goodness me' and 'Oh wow, we are trendy'.

'You're now being transported to a scene you're quite familiar with,' said Billy. On the VR screen the parents watched a family about to wake up. As they moved their heads in the devices, they could look around the bedroom and see two parents, who were suddenly rudely awoken by a blaring alarm clock.

'Goodness me!' blurted Dominic, who was having a far-above-average amount of fun for a regular Saturday.

As the parents watched, they saw the family rush around getting ready for the school day. 'Get up! You're going to be late for the bus!' shouted the mum in the video, who then sprinted down the stairs to put on some toast. **'WHERE ARE MY SHOES?'** yelled a voice from upstairs, which disturbed a baby in the other room, who started screaming. As the mum attempted to go back up the stairs, the smoke alarm began beeping and a dog burst out of the room, paused and did a little wee on the carpet. The video suddenly cut to black.

'Look familiar?' asked Billy Clarkson, bringing the parents back to reality.

'Oh yes, almost as stressful as our school run!' said Mel's mum, who found normal reality quite intense and probably didn't need a dose of virtual reality to deal with as well.

'Now watch this: your morning with your kids at **Rubbslings School for Creators and Influencers,'** Billy said, hitting play on a video that appeared to start very similarly to the first.

'There you are, look, and what time does it say on the clock? Nine a.m.! Wow, looks like you had a lie-in. Oh, and what's that? You even had time to do a little yoga, even read a few pages of your book,' said Billy, narrating the scenes with **CONFIDENCE.**

'And is that you checking the School Mums 'n' Dads group conversation to see how many problems there are? Nope, that group conversation doesn't even exist. Let's fast forward a bit. You're at a dinner party, you look well slept and glowing. You're telling everyone about how successful your kids are!' As Billy spoke these words, a terms and conditions box popped up on the VR screens. All of the parents skipped it.

He continued. 'Now you are video-calling your daughters. Is that on a new laptop provided to both you and your daughter by Rubbslings School for Creators and Influencers? Yes it is. You're all laughing; they are **excelling** because they are at the school of the future; you are excelling because you are great parents.'

The video faded to black and the parents began to remove their headsets.

Mel's mum raised her hand. 'How safe is this school? How diligent are the checks for beings with potentially monstrous defects?'

'A great question, Mrs Mel's Mum. Pop that headset back on.'

Back in virtual reality, the parents were floating over an island. They could see a castle, futuristic buildings, beaches. It all looked **VERY FANCY.**

'At the entrance of our island, we scan each and every student for monstrous defects . . . Plus, in action are our anti-monster-apparatus droids.'

The scene zoomed into the school courtyard as a virtual-reality student sprouted antlers, spider legs and a scorpion's tail. Within seconds, friendly-looking

white robots surrounded the beast, and the student was promptly neutralised with tranquilliser darts, captured and sealed in a giant red-and-white ball.

'It's top-of-the-range technology and the island's location makes it the safest school in the entire country.'

'Well, that really was something,' said Dominic. The virtual reality trip had seemed to briefly remind him what fun was.

'You're telling me!' said Jenners's mum. 'I could get on board with a place that gives us that life back.'

Sarah, who was not one to usually squash excitement but also was good at spotting problems, interrupted with her trademark reality pie. 'This is all very well and good but the girls already have their school places secured for September.'

'An absolutely valid point, Sarah. I'm glad you asked – I was just going to tell you about this,' said Billy, who absolutely hadn't been going to mention it unless somebody asked. 'Rubbslings is approved by the Educational Authority Board, to the highest rating

actually. Swapping your girls'
school places is much like swapping
that room-temperature beverage in front
of you for a new, ice-cold one,' Billy snapped at a
passing waiter. 'We will take care of everything.'

The mums and Dominic nodded and all made
approving faces before handing over their lukewarm
drinks to the waiter. **ONLY SARAH LOOKED UNSURE.**

Billy moved in for the kill. 'Oh, and did I mention
all four girls qualify for a **full scholarship** and all
school supplies are provided?'

He let this sit for a moment.

'I'll just leave these entry forms here. But don't take
too long to decide. The scholarship places are very
limited and there's a long waiting list.'

HE SAT BACK AND SMILED.

*

On this rare occasion, Jamie's Saturday had been less
exciting than her mum and Dominic's. There'd been
no virtual reality experiences for her but just dull old

normal reality at the thought of going to school without her best friends. She'd had dinner on her bed, checking for any Uncle-Barry-related news. Buttons lay on her pillow and poked at a leftover potato smiley face while feeling very potato sad face.

'Knock knock,' Sarah said out loud because Jamie's door was always open. 'Can I talk to you, dear?'

Jamie rolled over. 'Yeah . . . but I know what you're going to say.'

'Well, listen, we all had a good chat today. Sometimes you have to give us grown-ups a bit of extra time to understand new things.'

Jamie furrowed her brow and opened her eyes to look at her mum.

'Now I can't say I fully understand it all, or even agree with all of it but I can at least see how you will learn something useful,' said Sarah, who was making a conscious effort to give Jamie more responsibility after the summer that had been. 'Plus, the technology the school has makes it one of the safest places in the entire country. Part of being a good parent is knowing when to stop parenting. If you're sure this is the right decision . . .' Sarah gave her daughter's hand a little squeeze.

'I think so,' Jamie replied, squeezing back even harder. 'We've all talked about it a lot and we really think it's what we want to do.'

'Well, you've proved you're more responsible than most of the people in this house already, so if it's what you think is right, **I'm right behind you,'** Sarah said, and Jamie immediately reached out for a mum hug that always lasts that extra bit longer. 'Besides, I sort of hoped you hadn't changed your mind because Gercules and Mel's mum have already said yes too.'

'Really?' Jamie asked, her brain filling with the feeling you get when your parents say yes to a sleepover but times **A MILLION.** Buttons sensed some impending excitement and started spinning around repeatedly.

'Thank you, thank you, thank you, thank you!' Jamie went in for four repeated squeezes.

'OK, OK!' Sarah laughed. 'Well, you'd better make yourself useful before you leave Henrik to fend for himself here.'

Jamie instantly felt a wave of slight sadness. She hadn't connected that staying with her friends meant saying goodbye to her family, which included Henrik and Buttons, even if it was just for a little while, and also her mum after the two of them had been through so much. She even felt a peppering of sadness about Grandma, garnished by a twinge of worry that Uncle Barry was still out there somewhere . . .

'Are you all going to be OK?' asked Jamie.

'We'll be fine. Henrik is here, plus nobody's going to mess with your grandma. You'll get a new phone when you arrive and they're giving us a laptop so we can stay in touch,' said Sarah. 'Make sure you check in with Henrik, though – he'll be sad to see you go.'

'I'll tell him tomorrow,' Jamie said with a smile.

'Good idea. Right, now come and help me make some cups of tea. Your grandma will be getting **cranky** if she doesn't have number eight of the day.'

CHAPTER 10
140 PER CENT PURE BOAT

The early-morning sun was bright but there was a light breeze in the air. The girls were gathered on the Failsea & Crudwell station platform, suitcases in hand, chattering **EXCITEDLY.** The mums – Sarah, Chandice and Mel's mum – mumbled sleepily as Gercules talked them through her last wrestling match.

'Mum, you promised you wouldn't take the championship belt outside,' said Jenners, cringing with embarrassment.

'Important for everyone to know who the champ is,' Gercules said **GRUFFLY,** adjusting the big, heavy gold strap on her shoulder.

The train journey, apart from someone sitting in Chandice's reserved seat, was largely uneventful.

Which is lucky really because the aquatic experience is mad and we need plenty of book space to describe it appropriately.

The train pulled up at Sheringham Harbour station, which was one of those weird **MASSIVE** stations where every vehicle ever seemed to hang out. There were signs for taxis, buses, airport, trains, trams, bicycles, but annoyingly nothing for **AQUATIC EXPERIENCE VESSELS.**

The mums got in a decent amount of grumbling at this point:

'Well, you'd think they'd improve the signage in such a busy station.'

'It's a good thing we're not in a hurry.'

'I'll have to mention this on my Google review.'

Jamie looked around for clues and spotted a similar group of girls who were walking and talking into a phone. 'Let's follow them,' she said.

As usual, Jamie's instincts proved correct as the girls followed the group to Sheringham dock and looked up at what was hands down the largest boat they had ever seen. Jamie's insides were beginning to tingle. This was all starting to feel very real now.

'This is the boat to school?! We need to get a photo. A BOAT-O!' said Daisy, who always had an eye for content.

'It looks like a cut-in-half sea rocket,' said Mel, who has done our describing job for us. The boat looked 60 per cent **FUTURISTIC** and 80 per cent fancy, which makes 140 per cent but is about right because the boat was humongous. It must've been a thousand metres long as it jutted out into the ocean. Everything about it screamed **'LOOK HOW EXPENSIVE I AM'**, including its space-grey matte exterior. It had three tiered decks, on top of which sat an Olympic-sized swimming pool alongside a basketball court, which doubled up as a short tennis court like playgrounds at school. Unlike playgrounds at school, there were no chalked-out hopscotch squares but instead a helicopter landing pad.

The girls turned and said their goodbyes to the mums, who were super emotional but far less interesting than this big mad boat. The other students

were starting to arrive thick and fast, so Jamie led the girls up the gangway to the grand boat entrance, which probably has a more official, boaty sort of name, but

no one knew what it was. Once aboard, Jamie and the girls gathered at the top of a spiral staircase, which some other creators had already started sliding down.

'Can't slide down that staircase with these suitcases,' Jenners rightfully pointed out. So they got in the nearby queue to dump their luggage.

'Excuse me,' came a nervous voice from behind them. **'Are you Jamie McFlair?'**

The voice was from a boy whose hair was floppy but whose style choices were solid. His shirt was covered in **SHIMMERING** blue sequins and frills on the sleeves. He wore a matching blue neckerchief and black buckled boots. 'I'm Percival. I run a multi-platform showbiz brand. Super psyched to see you guys. I did like a whole series of videos about you at the World Music Festival. **You girls are super awesome.** Are you nervous? I'm quite nervous. I don't know anyone. So cool that you're the first people I've met!' Jamie took a moment to process that Percival had essentially vomited his entire life story into her brain, but her instinct was to look after him.

'That sounds cool! Lovely to meet you, Percival. You can hang out with us if you like?'

'Yay!' Percival **SQUEALED,** and then did another squeal as Jenners whizzed away down the rail of the spiral staircase shortly followed by Daisy. 'Can't believe I've seen Jenners!' he yelled.

'Would you like to slide or walk down the stairs, Mel?' asked Jamie.

'Walk down, please,' said Mel, who had been anxious about being made to slide for the whole suitcase queue.

The stairs led downstairs to a grand area that was essentially a **POSH DISCO AQUARIUM.** The walls were lined by tall tanks full of colourful fish that Jamie recognised from animated films. Neon lights shone overhead and the room was full of humans who looked just as varied and vibrant as the fish.

Before they had looked at one fish or danced to one verse of 'Breaktime Girlfriend', Jamie had met a girl called **PLUMSQUASH,** who had a YouTube channel about farming; **HOWDY BOW-WOW,** a popular dog from Instagram; the **CLONKER FAMILY,** who vlogged about their seemingly awesome life; and a chef called **ROUSHAN,** who made all of his meals from giant vegetables. Everyone was super friendly because they were literally all in the same boat and although they all made very different content, they were happy that they were among people who were all a bit weird, just like them. Everyone had their own unique thing going on. Jamie started to question what her **'THING'** was. *We* know it's foiling the plans of music moguls and slaying monsters, but even when you have an entire back catalogue of great success, brains can sometimes trick you and make you feel worried in new situations.

The group pressed their faces against the glass of the aquarium.

'It is quite weird that they have an aquarium on

a boat that is literally in the sea, which is basically just a giant aquarium,' said Mel, who slightly confused herself.

The whole group burst out laughing.

'Hahaha . . . Wait, say that again, I need to get that on camera,' said Plumsquash.

Mel wasn't used to other people laughing at her jokes in real life. 'Big boats full of internet people are very fun,' said Mel and everyone cheered. Jamie was smiling **EAR TO EAR.** This was a far cry from the rumours of how people treated Year 7s at Mel's original school.

Next stop was the pool, and the girls went to find deckchairs to sit on. A dancing purple dinosaur was handing out free, delicious lollies. Jenners grabbed several for the group, holding a lolly stick between each finger like ice-cream Wolverine.

Percival plonked himself on a deckchair next to Jamie.

'So psyched that we're going to be in the same class!' he said.

Jamie noticed there were bits of fluff sprouting from his chin similar to the fuzz you sometimes find on sad oranges.

'I think you're probably a bit older than us,' said Jamie. 'Unless they put different year groups in the same class?'

'Year groups? Oh em gee, that's so normal-people school!' Percival said with a laugh. 'Hey, Plumsquash! These girls thought Rubbslings had year groups based on age!?'

Plumsquash, who had purple hair and a round, friendly face, gave a giggle.

'Oh, hens,' she said with a thick Northern twang, not unkindly. 'Everyone's sorted into classes based on **how many followers they have.** You move up a class once you reach a certain number of followers.'

'So yeah, me and you, Jamie, we'll be in Class 0–10K,' said Percival. 'Plumsquash will be in the class above, but hopefully not for long because the school will teach us how to **grow our audiences.** We're coming to get ya, you rascal!' The pair giggled.

Jamie forced a laugh. Her brain was releasing a few drips of anxiety. She had visualised her, Daisy, Jenners and Mel all walking to class together, working on their VR homework together. Daisy and Mel had loads of followers. They were definitely not going to be in her class.

'Talk to you guys later!' said Jamie as she hurried to find Jenners, who had wandered off and found herself in the middle of a lolly-based TikTok dance-off. Jamie hauled her friend to safety and they moved to a quieter part of the deck.

'I think we're going to be in different classes,' said Jamie.

'How'd you work that one out?' said Jenners.

'Apparently they put us in classes based on our added-up followers. I've only got 6,925 so I'll be in Class 0–10K. You've got 10,003 so you'll be in the next class up from that. Then Daisy and Mel have both got way more than both of us so they'll be in a totally different class.'

'What a stupid way to decide classes,' said Jenners. 'I don't want to be in a class on my own. Don't worry, **I'VE GOT A PLAN.** Hold these lollies.'

Jenners pulled out her phone just as a flash of pink burst on to the scene.

'Well, LOOK who we have here,' the girl said, followed by a shrill squeal.

Jamie and Jenners couldn't believe who was standing in front of them.

SABRINA GUMBEAR was one of the biggest names on the internet. She had electric-pink hair and every movement seemed like a dance move. She was squealing at Jamie, who didn't have it in her soul to squeal back so just said, 'Ohh! Hi!'

'Jamie McFlair, **MONSTER SLAYER!** I'm super glad you're here! I am GASPING,' said Sabrina.

'Thanks!' said Jamie, who hadn't even introduced herself.

'OH! You should come hang out with us – we

could do a **dance/sketch mash-up collab** with some thrown underpants if you're up for that? I bet our audiences will WHEEZE!'

'Sure . . . that sounds great!' said Jamie, doing a bad job at sounding sure.

Sabrina squealed loudly and clapped her hands together really fast.

'I'm going to tell Martina and Yasmin that Jamie's

in **Team Gumbear.** They will FAINT! Catch ya later!' And she pirouetted, clicked her heels and started moonwalking away.

Jamie looked at Jenners.

'Sabrina Gumbear, there. Who everyone in school wanted to be, asking you to be in Team Gumbear. No big deal!' said Jenners, trying not to laugh.

'What is going on?' Jamie laughed.

'This place is mad,' said Jenners. 'Good news, I've already lost 215 followers – we're gonna be in the same class!'

'YAYYYYY.' Jamie gave Jenners a squeeze. 'What did you do?'

Jenners looked slightly guilty. 'I posted saying "dogs are going extinct", really annoyed a lot of people . . . and dogs aren't going extinct . . . so let's celebrate that at the boat disco.'

CHAPTER 11

NOTHING TO DECLARE BUT MY FOLLOWERS

Mel's first boat trip had taken a turn. 'Am I green? I feel like I'm green?' she asked the rest of the girls, desperately trying to only let words and not **VOMIT** out of her mouth.

'NAH, you're fine!' said Jenners as she gave her a friendly whack on the back, which made Mel's already delicate insides unstable. 'Hold it in, we're almost there now. I can see the island. Looks well weird from here, though.'

The island was coming into view. Jamie could make out the pebbly beach, and some odd-shaped buildings.

'Has anyone seen the goose?' asked Mel. The goose had not been seen since Jenners's lolly-based dance-off.

Before anyone could answer, an unnecessarily loud foghorn blared out from the top deck, which crossed

Mel's eyes.

'Think that means it's all going to be over now, Mel,' said Jamie, who had her arm round her queasy chum. **'I'm sure the goose will turn up,'** she added, unconcerned, anticipating that this goose may be on the loose for the second story in a row . . .

As the ship drifted towards the beach, everyone rushed into the stairwell in the opposite of a calm and orderly fashion. The excitement was at fever pitch and Jamie, Jenners, Daisy and Mel struggled to stay together.

'Hello, creators!'

Jamie turned to find a young man dressed in beach-professional attire: non-Hawaiian shorts, short-sleeved shirt with jazzy bow tie, and swinging a small microphone. Jamie thought she recognised him from somewhere . . .

'Welcome to Rubbslings! You guys are gonna have a fab time! Once you pass through these fancy gates, follow the path to our special scanners, which will allocate you to your class. These aren't based on age

but your subscriber count. Everyone happy with that?'

Another cheer rose up and the crowd started to excitedly shuffle through the grand cast-iron gate that stood proudly overhead. It had the words: RUBBSLINGS SCHOOL – YOUR PATH TO VIRTUAL HAPPINESS STARTS HERE moulded into the metal in a fancy font. Jamie briefly pondered whether virtual happiness was the same as real-life happiness.

The scanners were quick and the girls weren't waiting long, which was ideal as Jamie thought she felt a spot of rain. This was by no means a tropical island paradise. One by one, influencers of all shapes and sizes got rounded up by fancily dressed staff.

'Hello, guys,' said another vaguely recognisable young man. 'Daisy Palmer, Melissa Grainger . . . welcome to Rubbslings School. Our early readings show that you're going to be in Class 500K+! **Congratulations.**'

'SEE YOU IN THERE!' yelled Jenners, whose outdoor beach voice rivalled the volume of the boat **FOGHORN.**

'You know that feeling when you think someone is a someone but you don't know why? I just feel that with everyone I've seen today. Not sure if I'm supposed to recognise people or not,' said Jamie as Daisy and Mel were taken to a scanner.

It had definitely made chatting to people on the boat weird. Some people's names she knew already but she felt she had to pretend she didn't know, in order to have a normal interaction.

'McFlair, Jamie! Tregland, Jennifer! You're up next!' came the stern instruction from a security man who looked like he had **A DEGREE IN SQUASHING DREAMS.** 'Place your belongings on the conveyor belt and walk through the scanner, please.'

Jamie stepped forward to the scanner, where a friendly-looking lady gave her a wave.

'OK, Miss McFlair, if you could just hand us over your telephonic communications device for scannage?'

Jamie looked confused.

'Your phone, love,' said the scanning lady. Jamie handed it over. 'OK, just scanning that for you now . . . All clear! 6,925 total followers, minus a few inactive ones, a small number of bots but nothing to worry about . . . OK, so all students are eligible for a free upgrade on their device to a top-of-the-range *BananaPhone X16L Smiley Face Emoji*. All your data will be transferred automatically, which will take me no time at all. Shall I do that for you now?'

Jamie nodded as hard as she could. Even with the modest amount of money her mum got from the Big Time estate, she still would never have been able to justify a **TOP-OF-THE-RANGE BANANAPHONE.**

'OK, so you have been assigned to Class 0–10K. It's the bottom class, but don't worry you'll still have a lot of fun. Remember, the more followers you get, the higher up the school you move! I've set your phone up with **Class 0–10K privileges.** A full list of these will be in your student portal. But for today, as a welcome, all privileges are open to everyone until 6 p.m.! There is transport waiting over there, which will take you to the main school building. There will be free food and drink, and then a ceremony where you will be assigned a class tutor. Then you will go to your rooms, where you can explore a full catalogue of furnishings, gadgets and decorations, which will be delivered to your door within twenty-five minutes.'

Jamie was floored. She couldn't believe her luck. She'd managed to find herself at the best school in the world, which gave out free phones, and she was with her best friends. Getting a new phone is always a great day, especially when it's already set up. She scrolled through the student portal, looking at the tutors, wondering who she would get.

CHAPTER 12

RUBBSLINGS SCHOOL FOR CREATORS AND INFLUENCERS

With year groups assigned, phones upgraded and the goose still missing, Jamie and Jenners, along with the other creators, were bundled into a fleet of golf carts and taken towards the school. The last time Jamie had been in a golf cart was when she and Grandma used to race the old ones Barry had left behind in the mansion.

The main building looked like a **MASSIVE WEDDING CAKE** built out of space Lego. The top tier was made of mirrored glass, and the walls were covered in shimmering LED panels that flicked from red to green to gold. The other buildings looked like something you'd build when you ran out of proper Lego pieces.

A large brick building loomed behind ominously, and there was a castle that looked like it had been stolen from a **SPOOKY FAIRY TALE.**

The golf carts rolled over a bumpy metal bridge and crunched to a slow stop on the pebbly entrance to the main school building. Even though the first day hadn't started, everyone seemed to be rushing about back and forth, filming on their phones. White robots with **FRIENDLY FACES** rumbled and wheeled around, greeting new students by dispensing bags of pick'n'mix. Jamie could tell all of these things were about to blow Jenners's mind.

'Everyone's going to the canteen! We need to assess the snack situation! Plus make the most of our free privileges! We need to find Daisy and Mel too!' yelled Jenners, getting her priorities the wrong way round. She grabbed Jamie's arm a little too tightly and hoisted her along.

A loud bassy drone then rattled through the gaggle of colourful people and golf buggies. A deep, velvety voice rumbled into everyone's ears. **'RUBBSLINGS SCHOOL FOR CREATORS AND INFLUENCERS IS NOW ... OPEN!'** The front doors opened with an unnecessary amount of dry ice.

Everyone piled into the building, which was well air-conditioned and smelt of new carpet. They were ushered towards the canteen. The walls were filled with strange slogans like:

WELCOME TO VIRTUAL PERFECTION
STUFF = HAPPINESS
CONTROVERSY = CLICKS
IF IN DOUBT, ALWAYS POST ANYWAY

Jamie stared at the posters. There was something familiar about one of them, but she couldn't work out where from . . .

Rubbslings School's canteen was a strange cross between an all-you-can-eat restaurant and what Jamie imagined a nightclub would look like. At one end flashed a big neon sign saying **ORDER HERE.** On either side, lining the canteen, were large glass rooms, each lit in a different bold colour.

Jamie thought she was pretty grown-up for her age. She knew things about coding and website building that people in university struggled with. She also had a lot of respect for people's feelings even though she could get quite hot-headed at times. But there was no way her brain could sensibly deal with this all-you-can-eat, delicious food free-for-all, and she wasn't alone.

During the frenzy of plate-piling, Jamie finally saw Mel, which brought her back to her senses. Mel was standing still, **CONFUSED,** holding a tray with chips and pizza covered in blue slushy, beans and chocolate sprinkles.

'I think I need to start again . . .' she said glumly.

Jamie then spotted Daisy, who was with Sabrina Gumbear.

'Hey, Daisy! Hey, Sabrina, do you guys want to come sit with us?' said Jamie excitedly. 'You should see Mel's food, **it's hilarious.'**

'Classic Mel!' said Daisy, smiling.

Sabrina, who had been all smiles on the boat, now seemed frosty.

'Aren't these guys in Class 0–10K, though?' she said, as if Jamie had turned into a dog's bottom surprise since they'd last spoken.

'You should come sit with the other Class 500K+s, Dais. You should meet SandwichSays. He's cool, doing BIG numbers and he will make you GLOW!'

Daisy looked like she was being made to choose whether to **DELETE PUPPIES OR TO DELETE KITTENS FROM EXISTENCE.** Her eyes were darting between Jamie, who was fuming, and Sabrina, who was pouting rhythmically.

'I'm going to eat with my friends from my old school, Sab. But I'll catch you later.'

Sabrina looked unimpressed and tap-danced away. Jamie could tell Daisy was disappointed.

'That was awkward . . .' said Daisy.

'She was really nice on the boat?!' said Jamie, who was both regular-annoyed and also annoyed because she was hungry.

'Could you imagine if she said that to Jenners, though?' said Mel, who then did a Jenzilla impression.

This made Jamie and Daisy laugh.

In a tradition that had carried over from their days at junior school, Jenners was saving the seats. The four sat, eating heartily, discussing how they would decorate their rooms, who their tutors could possibly be, and Jenners explained to Mel how to create the perfect buffet plate.

Jamie looked around at the scene: her friends chomping happily and the weird and wonderful, colourful people that surrounded her, and, perched outside the window of the canteen, a strange mechanical parrot that shimmered from blue to gold.

'*BWARK!*'

CHAPTER 13
MOVE TO THE AL G RHYTHM

With their tummies full of everything other than essential nutrients, Jamie and the girls made their way to the assembly hall. If you didn't go to a school secretly built by an evil genius, you may be picturing a school gym or a big room with lots of **UNCOMFORTABLE CHAIRS** facing a bleak-looking stage. Well, the Rubbslings assembly hall was more like a futuristic mega-theatre. There were no teachers lining the sides, but instead a line of face scanners at the entrance, which shone an infrared light at you, bleeped and told you your seat number.

'WELCOME . . . JA . . . MIE   MC . . . FLAIR . . . YOUR SEAT IS FLOOR IN TIER F,' the machine blurted. **'WELCOME . . . ME . . . LISS . . . UH . . . GRAINGER . . . YOUR SEAT IS LUXURY EGG CHAIR IN TIER A.'**

'Looks like I've got to head upstairs . . .' said Mel

nervously, ignoring the news about the luxury egg chair.

'Don't worry, Mel, Daisy will be upstairs too!' said Jamie reassuringly. 'And I've got Jenners so I'll be fine.'

'Whoever is sitting next to you is moving,' said Jenners, who would be sitting down next to her best friend at all costs. **'I'm full of flapjack and I will crush them.'**

In the centre of the room, hundreds of tiny screens wrapped around a huge, luminous globe. It filled the whole space with light and on its surface a clock was counting down. The whole thing was more space station than school assembly hall.

Jamie and Jenners wandered across the shiny white marble floor towards their section roped off as TIER F and found a spot by Percival, who was on a livestream babbling tuneful nonsense. The marble floor was uncompromising on their backsides.

'Buzzing for this!' Percival's head and phone popped between Jamie and Jenners. 'I asked some

Class 250–500K students, and they say the tutor line-up is pretty unreal! They also think Sabrina Gumbear is secretly WORKING FOR THE SCHOOL! **AND** there might be some massive prank played on students so to be on your guard,' he garbled, without pausing to take a breath.

'Just here with two of my best friends, Jamie and . . . Jenster . . . Say hi to the chat, girls!'

'It's Jenners,' interrupted Jenners.

'Classic Jenster . . . We're in the assembly hall waiting to hear from the headmaster . . . Look how crazy modern this place is . . . Oh, AND we're gonna find out who our class tutors are . . . Ahh, it's starting . . . I'll update you . . .' Percival stopped recording as the final few students scrambled to their seats and chit-chat was drowned out by thumping, dramatic music.

The lights in the room dimmed to black. Psychedelic graphics began zipping around the screens of the giant globe, bursting into colour like a **DIGITAL FIREWORK DISPLAY,** the music ramped up and the atmosphere grew.

'ELITE STUDENTS OF RUBBSLINGS SCHOOL FOR CREATORS AND INFLUENCERS,' boomed the velvety voiceover man from earlier. 'PLEASE WELCOME THE ARCHITECT, THE INVENTOR, YOUR HEADMASTER . . . **AL G RHYTHM!**'

Deafening applause mixed with deafening drum and bass filled the assembly hall. There were cheers and shouts as the hundreds of tiny screens formed a face, which repeated in all directions around the light globe.

'Yes, yes, yes, what's going on!'

The face had tightly cropped curly hair and what Grandma would call **A MILLION-DOLLAR SMILE.**

'You guys like that boomy voice I was doing earlier? Sounded like a proper bossman!' The room laughed. Unsurprisingly, this headmaster wasn't like anything the girls had ever experienced. Jamie wasn't sure if she was supposed to recognise him, but he had very distinct mannerisms and unique eyebrow behaviour that **SHE RECOGNISED FROM SOMEWHERE.**

'Welcome, I'm Al G Rhythm – you can call me Professor Rhythm! Welcome to your future. You have been chosen to lead the world in the ways of the internet. With our creative guidance, you will be the **most advanced minds on the planet!** As you work your way up the classes, your opportunities improve! The more content you make, the quicker you will grow your audiences!'

The applause erupted once again.

'Now, listen up, yeah, because Rubbslings is an elite academy. People are begging for a place here! I know you guys won't let us down, but we don't want no dead channels here, do we guys!'

A big 'NO' rang out from the crowd.

'If we see them follower numbers falling, you could see yourself outta here! Drop-kicked back into reality! No more privileges! No more free stuff! So don't drop the ball, gang! **Keep that audience growing!'**

More cheers, even bigger than before. Jamie and

Jenners exchanged an awkward glance.

'We want you to use the whole island to inspire and create. HOWEVER, the castle is out of bounds to all except successful graduates and really important teachers. Also, don't be sneaking into the Cliffside Camp as it's home to the island's native tribe and they might get sweaty. Gotta respect their wishes to not be disturbed. **Also, cliffs are bare dangerous.'**

Jamie immediately made a mental note to try and visit these places.

'BUT NOW IT'S TIME FOR THE TUTOR REVEAL!'

The pulsing drum and bass was back. Lasers filled the building and explosions of pyrotechnics caused both Jenners and Jamie to violently jump. Jamie worried whether Mel was coping with all this fuss.

'Creators! Please go wild for the first tutor . . . For Class 500K+ . . . **TOBYISSOCOOLLIKE!'**

A door opened beneath the globe and a slender bespectacled fellow awkwardly stepped through the dry ice waving to the roaring crowd.

'TobyIsSoCoolLike, from ORIGINAL YouTube days!' said Jamie.

'That's him!' Jenners's head swivelled. 'Mel and Daisy are well lucky!'

'For Class 250–500K, please welcome, **Ally B!!**'

A cheer rose from the crowd. Ally B first shot to fame playing football video games but then became a semi-successful mainstream grime artist.

'For Class 100–250K . . .' boomed the headmaster's voice, 'it's **Spacey HighHat!!**' The first ever YouTuber to hit one million subscribers emerged from the globe, dancing and waving.

Class 50–100K got the streamer **Bartiplier,** Class 10–50K got **Mr Creatures,** and finally . . .

Jenners, Jamie and Percival looked at each other with crossed fingers.

'CREATORS, please welcome the tutor for Class 0–10K . . . **StompyDog!!**'

JAMIE AND JENNERS EXPLODED.

'Oh my days, oh my days, oh my days . . .' said Jamie, who had found herself in a cheering huddle with Jenners and Percival. 'I used to watch him ALL the time as a kid! He basically was my parents.'

'He hasn't uploaded in like eight months so I thought he was dead! **This is much better news!**' roared Jenners.

StompyDog videos had been Jamie's early childhood. He felt like an older brother and remembering his Minecraft adventures was filling her soul with warm nostalgia. She knew Jenners would feel the same. The girls felt like they owed StompyDog for their friendship.

CHAPTER 14

THE WORLD'S COOLEST TUTOR

This is the weirdest classroom in history, thought Jamie as she clambered out of the ball pit, shortly followed by a loud, colourful **PLASTIC EXPLOSION** as Jenners followed Jamie down the slide.

She and Jenners were the last to arrive, and hurried to take the two remaining chairs. Describing these seating objects as chairs doesn't really do them justice. One was like a giant egg filled with pillows, which Jenners squeezed herself into. The other was plastic but filled with juice and fruits. Jamie delicately perched herself on the edge but fell back in the wobbliness.

'Do you think he's actually real? Do you think he'll notice us? Do you think he'll know we've been subscribers since we were four?' blurted Jamie in a rare, freak-out-induced word vomit. 'I can't believe he's our **TEACHER!**' she announced, forgetting to use the appropriate indoor voice that grown-ups like.

'I KNOW!' yelled Jenners in a voice that was definitely meant for stadiums, not classrooms, before immediately starting a Mexican wave that rippled round the room and merged into a chant of 'Stompy . . . Dog, Stompy . . . Dog!'

The classroom door swung open with force and banged against the wall.

'WHAT is going on in here?' said a man in a big, brown dog onesie. He had a head of big, bouncy curls and a T-shirt with a Minecraft axe on it.

He glared at the class intensely, who fell immediately silent.

'If you're going to chant in my classroom . . . you need to **BANG** the tables as well! No point doing it if you're not going to do it properly!' he said as the class erupted into an even louder StompyDog chant than before.

'That's better!' yelled Stompy over the cheers. 'Oh, this is going to be a fun term. My name is StompyDog,

for anyone who may have forgotten me,' he said, scribing it on to the smartboard, 'and I shall be your form teacher while you remain in Class 0–10K here at Rubbslings School for Creators and Influencers.'

THE CLASS GIGGLED. 'We know who you are, sir!' said Percival, whose arm uncontrollably shot up into the air. 'I was a subscriber when you only had a thousand subs!'

StompyDog chuckled. 'An original fan! We love to see it! Hey, and don't worry about the hand-raising "sir" stuff, dude! We're all friends here. This is not like your normal school. We do things **differently** here! We want you to be yourself, be different, be weird!'

The class was hanging on every sing-songy word.

'In fact, before I made my own channel, I was a fan just like you guys! Don't tell him, but I actually started a fansite about Bartiplier, who's a teacher here too!'

'I used to do that for BNA!' blurted Jamie excitedly. She'd always

160

thought she was the only person to really do stuff like that.

'What's your name?'

'Jamie McFlair,' said Jamie McFlair.

'Dude, seriously? I'm Jamie McFlair's tutor? Actual real-life **monster slayer** Jamie McFlair. Holy moly, that is so awesome, and I'm guessing that's Jenners next to you,' said Stompy with a point.

'That's my name, don't wear it out!' shouted Jenners as Stompy laughed. Both she and Jamie were swelling with **PRIDE.** Actual StompyDog knew their names!

Stompy clapped his hands. 'Hey, I knew we'd have some real talent in Class 0–10K! These other classes are going to learn what we're made of, right, gang?!'

The class cheered. Everyone started to excitedly share things they'd done and achieved. Could Jamie's Year 5 teacher Mrs Bloggins's spell as her all-time favourite teacher be coming to an end?

After sorting out some classic first day of school admin, Jamie and Jenners left StompyDog's classroom bouncing with excitement. But as they reached their student accommodation, their brain batteries hit 1 per cent. It had been a very long day. Jamie had never been so tired at only half past six in the evening. It felt like they had been on Failsea & Crudwell station platform a million years ago.

'Right, I'm in room 32B over here somewhere, apparently. What lessons do we have tomorrow?' said Jenners.

'Posing for Photos, Lip-Sync Skills, YouTube Drama, then History of Memes,' said Jamie, looking at the timetable on her phone.

'Ridiculous,' said Jenners. 'Well. Night!'

Jamie tapped her phone on the console next to her door as it slid open with a satisfying purr. Jamie's room was completely empty other than a bed, her suitcase and her new tablet, which didn't have a case or even a screen protector. Picking up expensive things without cases on always made her feel uneasy. She sat on the bed and logged on to the student portal.

'Have YOU ever wanted to hang out with someone more famous than you? How about

being friends with your favourite A-lister? Upgrade your circle of friends with VR Celebz Version 5.2 . . . Recently added celebz include: Lady Day, Nica Konstantopolous and television's Will Kelly! Plus sign up now to receive your FREE Rachael Ladadaygee skin . . . Find us on the Rubbslings portal today!'

Jamie waited for the five-second ad timer to count down so she could skip it, finally getting to the portal homepage.

TRENDING TOPICS: #SLIME #TUNESINCOSTUMES #BANANANAN3 #HUNPALOOZA #JACKLARSSONISOVER #AXELLARSSON #PUDDINGS #RABBIT #TRANSFERDEADLINE #FAMARAPLEASESTAY

Jamie tapped on 'Store'. She scrolled through page after page. There were different cameras, phones, smart speakers, room decorations. She saw a pug lamp that reminded her of Buttons; she tapped immediately to purchase.

Error – this item is only available for those in Class 10–50K and above.

That's annoying, said Jamie's brain.

People who ordered this item also liked: pug rug.

Essential purchase! thought Jamie and tapped accordingly.

Error – this item is only available for those in Class 10–50K and above.

'What's this thing's problem?' Jamie shouted. This was getting silly. She chose an item at random and tapped 'Purchase'.

Error – this item is only available for those in Class 50–100K and above.

Literally 0 per cent of these items are available for my class – this is stupid! thought Jamie. She could only imagine how annoyed Jenners was getting and couldn't help but feel a tiny bit jealous that Mel and Daisy's rooms were probably filled with everything they could ever dream of. After half an hour of fruitless scrolling, she put the tablet down with a sigh.

She clicked open her suitcase. Underneath her **SLIME BLASTER,** which she'd brought in case of emergencies, she found her photo of Henrik and Buttons. It was of Buttons's fourth birthday at the beginning of summer, when Henrik had bought him a little dog fez so they could match. Jamie smiled. She already missed them and wondered what they were doing right that moment. With the last of her energy, Jamie threw herself on the bed and tapped out a long message to Mum, telling her about the day, asking about Henrik and Buttons and making sure Grandma and Sheamus were staying out of trouble. Seconds after she pressed send, she fell into a deep sleep.

She was so tired she didn't even notice the *tap tap tapp*ing of a metal beak on the outside of her room window.

'*BWARK!*'

CHAPTER 15
FUNDAY MORNING

When a grown-up asks, 'How has your first day at secondary school been?' a normal response might include, 'I'm getting on well with maths' or **'I'VE MADE A NEW FRIEND'**. In Jamie's case, there were far more bonkers occurrences to include. In the first lesson of the morning, Jenners had been asked to leave class for *not* being on her phone enough in Posing for Photos class, and in a double period of Lip-Sync Skills, Jamie had received a standing ovation for her presentation, mainly because she had chosen Scott's verse of a BNA tune to mime to.

As the school bell rang, which signalled the end of a particularly strange YouTube Drama lesson, Jamie got to her feet.

Jenners was waiting for her outside Monkey-Covering-Eyes Emoji classroom. Important to say here that all the classes at Rubbslings School were named after emojis. On paper this sounds cool but in reality is a really impractical way of remembering which classroom is which.

'I could see you fuming from across the room,' said Jenners.

'Yeah, that was all sorts of **nonsense,**' replied Jamie. 'Don't ever leave me in this class alone,' she said, as a new message notification popped on to her phone. She clicked to open it but an advert popped up first.

'Have YOU ever wanted to hang out with someone more famous than you? How about being friends with your favourite A-lister? Upgrade your circle of friends with VR Celebz Version 5.2 . . .'

'NO!' they both said in unison, as Jamie hammered the skip button for what seemed like the longest five seconds ever. Jamie pressed on the message again and this time it opened.

'MEL!' yelled Jamie as she saw her bouncing round the corner with a hat and backpack that were meant for adventuring outside. The two went for a full squeeze just as Jenners wrapped her arms round both of them and squeezed a little too hard.

'Daisy! Get in here!' shouted Jenners.

Daisy was a few metres behind Mel in a group of girls, the members of which were rivalling her fashion sense – a rare occurrence in Daisy-land. Jamie could spot Sabrina Gumbear's bubblegum-coloured hair in the crowd. Daisy looked up and acknowledged the girls with a nod.

'Sorry, guys, gotta dash!' she said before disappearing with the rest of Team Gumbear.

'We'll catch up with her later . . .' reassured Mel.

'If she can spare her precious time,' Jamie said. 'Why does she take so long to reply to the group messages too? She's literally on her phone all the time.' Jamie could feel her frustration growing. 'This school was supposed to keep us together, not make it even harder to see each—'

'Mel, your HAIR!' blurted Jenners, staring at Mel's head. Her hat had fallen off in the hug and her hair appeared to be giving off light, having been dyed a **LUMINOUS GREEN.**

'I know, right, TobyIsSoCoolLike said it would rate better with my audience, according to my analytics or something,' replied Mel, who deep down thought her hair looked like a Year 2 art project. 'To be fair, he has bleached his hair seventeen times on YouTube so he probably knows what he's doing, right?'

'Isn't he bald now?' asked Jenners.

Mel nodded nervously.

'Which is COOL, obviously,' Jenners said, realising she needed to immediately change the subject. 'What's he LIKE, though? Actual TobyIsSoCoolLike! I used to want to marry him!'

'He's been married three times!' said

Mel excitedly. 'His life sounds amazing!'

'Percival will be so excited to hear that,' said Jamie, then paused, realising she hadn't seen him all day. *Weird.*

One good thing about how mad the lessons at Rubbslings School were was that mornings would usually fly by and the girls trotted off to lunch discussing the **LATEST GOSSIP.** The most recent rumour going around the school was who would be chosen for the big creator boxing match. YouTubers in boxing matches had become a thing a few years ago and had started to become a strange internet tradition where the most popular YouTubers would face off for gazillions of views.

'Why can't they just do a sports day like a normal school, you know, run a race or something?' asked Jamie. 'A boxing match seems a bit much.'

'I'm not sure egg and spoon races get as many views,' said Mel. 'Definitely safer, though, at least for the person.

Very dangerous for the egg, of course.'

'Can you do **suplexes** in boxing?' asked Jenners.

'I don't think so,' replied Mel.

'Sounds boring,' said Jenners, who lifted a nervous Mel up off her feet and roared.

The three of them laughed and then hurried up because their tummies had also started roaring.

The canteen looked as mad as it had when they first arrived. In each of the glass areas, students were gobbling down lunches. On one side was a room filled with red light. In the next shone a bright green light, a yellow room and a pink . . .

'Daisy!' screeched Jenners. There sitting behind the glass, illuminated in pink and gobbling down a cavalcade of delicious-looking delights, was Daisy. Next to her, with a plate of equally fancy-looking treats and a drink with a curly straw in it, was Sabrina Gumbear. Jenners squashed her face up against the glass, **MAKING FISH MOUTHS.**

'Do you *know* her?' said Sabrina in a tone that suggested she was not a fan of fish mouths on glass, or just anything fun. 'Why is she doing that?'

Daisy started to turn red. 'Yeah, sort of, she went to my old school, **she's cool though.**'

'She doesn't look cool,' said Sabrina, who accidentally missed her drink with her straw and speared some garlic bread because she was wearing sunglasses inside.

Jamie placed her phone on the reader that read

SCAN HERE. She waited a couple of seconds, before the light above flashed red and said:

ERROR – THIS DINING AREA IS ONLY AVAILABLE FOR THOSE IN CLASS 500K+.

Daisy got up from the table and wandered to the door, which slid open. 'Weird . . . but hi! I'd come out and sit with you but I've already got my food.'

'Just bring it with you,' said Jenners impatiently. 'I'm starving; I can feel **Jenzilla brewing.'**

Jenzilla was what the girls called Jenners when she got quite angry or very hangry or a combination of the two. It would usually result in her entering a violent rage that was sometimes useful in emergencies.

'Ah, don't worry about me but go and grab your food! Definitely get the spaghetti, too – IT IS LUSH!' said Daisy.

'Let us in when we come back, yeah?' said Jamie.

'Yep . . . me and Sabrina have to shoot some

content but if I'm still here, sure,'

replied Daisy, who looked distracted.

'Fine,' said Jamie **BLUNTLY.**

'To be honest, Jenzilla is gonna break down the door anyway! Isn't that right, Jenzilla!' added Mel, who began chasing Jenners towards the food, roaring as she went. Jamie frowned at Daisy then ran after the others.

At the canteen bar there was no slightly disgruntled lunch person. Instead, they were greeted by a screen that read *Spaghetti bolognese – SCAN BELOW.* Jenners proceeded to hold her phone under the scanner, which bleeped.

'Have YOU ever wanted to hang out with someone more famous than you? How about being friends with your favourite A-lister? Upgrade your circle of friends with VR Celebz Version 5.2 . . .'

'Ads before food?!' said Jenners, outraged. 'That's where I draw the line.' She mashed the 'skip ad' button with her fist until a robot arm shot out from the wall holding a steaming plate of spaghetti. Jenners grabbed the plate from the metal arm. 'Hey, where's my sauce and bolognese? This is just pasta!'

'Hang on, I'll try it – you can have some of mine,' said Jamie, in the way that best friends do. She scanned her phone, then waited a second before the robot arm disappeared and shot back out with another plate of **UN-BOLOGNESED SPAGHETTI.**

'Right, I'm not having this,' said Jenners, on the precipice of erupting into Jenzilla mode. She slammed her hand down on the 'press for help' button.

'*Pshhhhh* . . . Yes what?' came the slightly irritated response from the speaker.

'Hi there, UM, we seem to only have spaghetti and no bolognese on our plates.' said Jenners in her voice that she saved for talking to adults.

'*Pshhh* . . . Students receive bolognese privileges in Class 10–50K,' blurted the speaker.

'What!? **Give me bolognese!** And where are knives and forks?' Jenners shouted.

'Students receive cutlery privileges in Class 10–50K . . . **Have a nice day** . . . *Pshhh*,' said the intercom, followed by a long dial tone, signalling there would be no more questions.

'Let me try,' said Mel, putting her phone under the scanner. This time the robot arm took a little longer and then produced a gourmet plate of spaghetti bolognese with sauce and meatballs, garnished with Parmesan, some green leaves, four chocolate brownies, after-dinner mints, a sparkler, a tiny paper flag with Mel's face on it, **A SHINING GOLD FORK, A SPOON AND A TENNER.**

'Whaat . . .' said Jenners, stunned, as the robot arm retracted and re-emerged with a gigantic cup of blue drink and plopped in a fun swirly straw.

'We'll share,' said Mel, clearly embarrassed.

When Jamie led the group back to the pink dining area, Daisy was gone. They joined the area where the rest of the 0–10K class sat on wooden benches eating plates of blank spaghetti with their bare hands.

'Nice to spend some quality time with you, Daisy. I'm fine, thanks, just eating spaghetti with my hands but at least we're all together . . . oh no, wait.' Jamie picked up a clump of spaghetti and let it sadly slop on to the plate.

'If we're being totally honest, we all know she's much cooler than us. I kind of expected the day when she'd move on,' said Jenners, dishing out some **HARSH TRUTHS.**

'No! We came here to stay together. If it's not the four of us then **what's the point?** Why are we even here?' said Jamie, pushing her plate away.

'I'll try and talk to her – maybe she doesn't even realise.' Mel plopped one of her meatballs on to Jamie's plate as Jenners leant over and helped herself to the remaining three.

Jamie smiled at her, then turned to the rest of the table. 'Have any of you seen Percival today?'

The other students looked blank. A small boy looked over at her and said, 'No, maybe he's with my friend Javed? Haven't seen him today either . . .'

Strange to miss so much first-day stuff, thought Jamie, grabbing another clump of spaghetti.

*

As the first week continued, Jamie felt an air of emptiness in her stomach. She was happy that at least she was **TECHNICALLY** still at school with her best friends but it didn't feel like it had at their old school. She felt jealous of Mel getting nicer food and that Daisy seemed to be making friends, even though she didn't really like them.

On the walk back to her room after an NFT art class, Jamie remembered that her favourite teacher at Crudwell School, Mrs Bloggins, had told her that going to secondary school might feel difficult at the beginning, but this wasn't just difficult; it was weird. **SUSPICIOUS,** even.

She thought about all the things she'd seen since arriving here. The extravagant boat and the welcome staff who seemed strangely familiar; the chaotic lessons and larger-than-life headmaster she'd only ever seen on-screen; the rigid rules around year group privileges and the crazy number of adverts she was **BOMBARDED** with. And where was Percival? She hadn't seen him for days and it was hard to miss someone whose shoes were so great, and was 99 per cent flamboyant yet 1 per cent annoying. She felt uneasy somehow.

Should she confide in Mr StompyDog? Or maybe tell her mum? She quickly dismissed the thought – after working so hard to convince her mum to let her go to this school, she couldn't let her think it wasn't perfect. Besides, her family seemed **TOO BUSY** to video call her at the moment – every time she tried to arrange something they asked to postpone. *No, this is something I need to tackle on my own.*

Jamie got out her old BNA notepad. Notepads are a lot like the notepad app on your phone, but you write the words with a pen on pages you can hold. Grandma always said to write your secrets down on paper so the government can't steal them. Usually she would ignore her shoe-throwing, wine-chugging, football hooligan grandma's advice, but something about doing things in an old-school way at this very new school seemed sensible.

She flicked past old designs of the BNAspace, the slime recipe for her slime blaster, her top ten favourite *Kid Ninja* moments, found a blank page and started listing down **WEIRD THINGS** she'd noticed at the school. Once she'd filled her third page, she knew she had to share her findings with the girls.

CHAPTER 16
SUPER BARRY-O-KART

'He's so slippery!' yelled Slottapuss, trying to keep hold of a gungy **WIGGLER** of a boy.

'*Aidez-moi! Je ne veux pas être un lapin,*' cried the boy, who used to be a multi-platform showbiz reporter in Class 0–10K but now, thanks to another unsuccessful test of Barry's **ULTIMATE BRAIN HACK,** thought he was a French rabbit. His wails were echoing around the stress carnival.

Barry stood at the Ultimate Control Console pinching the bridge of his nose hard. He had been CERTAIN he had the formula right this time.

'Get him out of my sight, Slottings,' yelled Barry. 'Take him to the Cliffside Camp for quarantine. If he keeps wriggling, give him a **BONK** on the head with the big red mallet. But be quick as we've got go-karting.'

Slottapuss gave a thumbs up. **'Come on, Mr Percival,'** he chimed as he bundled the floppy-haired wriggler into a heavy-duty refuse sack.

Barry's phone bleeped. It was a message from Top-Secret New Accomplice.

I'm at the go-kart track. Ready to ZOOM.

It had been essential that Barry was regularly entertained while locked away in the Barry Castle. A bored Barry Bigtime was arguably the most dangerous. A good portion of the Megacleese diamond booty had been spent on fully immersive VR playrooms, a paintballing arena, a pottery room and a full go-kart track. Over the last week Barry had been starting to feel cooped up and restless, like he was being forced to hide away from a highly contagious flu-like disease.

So Flobster had organised a race among Barry's inner circle around the castle go-kart track.

It wasn't far from the stress carnival. Inside the track, ready to race, stood Flobster, Proudy and Barry's top-secret new accomplice, whose identity was hidden behind their crash helmet.

'How'd the latest experiment go, Mr Bigtime?' asked Proudy cheerfully.

'**Badly,**' snapped Barry. 'Expect another bonkers student in your Cliffside Camp soon. And you!' Barry said, pointing at the crash-helmet person. 'Are you guiding my niece to the promised land of influencer greatness?'

'She is very resistant to the ways of the influencer,' came the muffled voice of the mystery person. 'She doesn't seem bothered by follower numbers, or by popular groups, or even making good content. She just seems to care quite deeply about her **friends.**'

Barry flounced.

'Boss, why don't we just throw her to the sharks and get it over with?' asked Flobster.

'Because, my abhorrent accomplice, the most important influencer in my influencer army will be **Jamie McFlair.** With her brain at my control, she will help **restore my name.** It's the perfect revenge! Then, obviously, I'll feed her to sharks after that,' added Barry. 'So you'd better do whatever it takes to make her build her following!' Barry said, rapping his knuckles on the top-secret new accomplice's helmet.

More repugnant chat followed as they waited for Slottapuss to join them.

'Right, that's all dealt with!' said Slottapuss as he arrived. 'I picked up some things on the way back from the camp that we can use in the race.' He handed out some **BANANA SKINS** and some empty turtle shells to the racers as they climbed into their karts.

There was some frantic **ZOOMING,** lots of evil chuckling and plenty of underhand karting behaviour. It was the last lap, and Barry was in second place. The

top-secret accomplice was quite the racer and making for the finish line. Barry had one last turtle shell in his lap, and with an insane amount of luck **PINGED** the shell right off the accomplice's head, knocking off their helmet and causing the kart to skid out into some tyres.

Barry blasted over the finishing line, whooping **TRIUMPHANTLY,** power-slid and turned to face the second-place loser.

'Ha. Surprised you could see anything at all with all that ridiculous hair in your eyes,' yelled Barry.

The accomplice looked up, pulling the sweaty, curly hair from his eyes.

'You got me, Mr Bigtime, sir. You got me,' came the sing-song voice of **STOMPYDOG.**

CHAPTER 17

THE ABDICATION OF QUEEN GNOME

The library was one of the few places in the school that reminded Jamie of home. It was also one of the few places that allowed access for all privilege levels, so it was the perfect place for her **SECRET GET-TOGETHER** with the others.

The room was laid out in booths, each with a big touch screen and what looked like a mini water slide underneath it. Ninety-nine per cent of books you could just download but every now and then there'd be one that was only in **REGULAR BOOK FORM.** If you ordered it, it would slide down the chute and you could scan it out.

'Over here!' whispered Jamie in her library voice, as she saw Mel and Jenners approaching. 'Wait for it to go past, though.'

A tall, white robot was roaming the perimeter of

the library. It had a deceptively **FRIENDLY FACE** and Jamie knew it slowly patrolled all the booths, checking that there was no suspicious activity occurring, like more than one person per booth.

'Flying saucers or pink shrimps?' Mel said as she snuck into the booth, offering up some sweets that were definitely not available to Jamie and Jenners's year group.

'Both.' Jenners grabbed a combo and popped them one by one in her gob.

'Where's Daisy?' asked Mel.

'Who knows?' said Jamie sadly.

This situation makes us sad too but to not include it would've been skipping over the truth. In the last week, Daisy had replied to only **TWO GROUP MESSAGES,** liked one Instagram post from Mel and not responded to a single DM from any of them.

Jamie opened the BNA notepad.

'Woah, paper! Old school!' said Jenners as Jamie

began to go through some of the weird things that she'd written down.

'The meal privileges, the classrooms that look like they've been designed by kids, that weird headmaster, Al G Rhythm, who no one seems to have ever heard of, **not even Google.** That Minecraft Javed kid in our class who was sent to the headmaster and never seen since. Also, has anyone seen Percival? It's not just me, is it?' asked Jamie in between chewy-shrimp mouthfuls. 'None of our families want to do video calls. Henrik keeps sending me pictures but they're all from months ago – it's weird.'

'This will sound strange,' said Jenners, her open mouth full of pink gloop. 'But Mum doesn't text like Mum any more. She's only ever used five emojis. Yesterday she sent the **otter on the log emoji.** It's quite a new one. Just felt odd to me.'

'Yeah, my brother has been sending me the same messages from weeks ago that make no sense,' said Mel, whose general level of confusion was at peak levels of late.

'Interesting,' said Jamie, who added *suspicious emoji usage* to her list.

'This content schedule is mad as well,' Jamie continued. 'I can't keep up.'

Jenners put her hand back in the bag to sweep up the UFO detritus. 'I'm trying to **LOSE** followers; I don't want to move out of our class without you. My last four videos were with this sock puppet I literally made as a joke.'

Jenners pulled out a white school sock from her pocket. It had two **GOOGLY EYES** and a bit of broken pencil stuck on for a mouth.

'The annoying thing is, the videos are performing **BETTER.** My followers voted for its name; I didn't even ask them to. He's called **Prince Alfred Dribblewater.** Nothing

makes any sense any more I swear.'

'I've got these four fans who comment hundreds of times on everything I do!' said Mel. 'They've even made a fan account for my sunhat.'

'Sounds like us and BNA,' chuckled Jenners.

'Were we *that* obsessed?' asked Jamie.

'I hacked into a police database just to find out what party they were going to . . . and ended up spending **two weeks in jail,**' said Jenners, licking sugar from her fingers. 'Then, me, Mel and Daisy stole old ladies' mobility scooters and your gran nicked a bus. **Don't kid yourself,** Jamie, we were out of control last year.'

Another seed sprouted in Jamie's brain. As much as she tried to squash the thoughts, the dread in her tummy was growing and it was dread she recognised from before.

'I'm going to message Scott,' said Jamie as she began scrolling through her contacts.

'He definitely owes us for, you know, essentially saving all their lives and careers,' said Jenners.

'Yeah, and he always said if you ever need me for anything just DM me,' replied Jamie.

'Girls, change booth!' came a whisper from behind them. It was Daisy! She pointed at the library patrol robot taking an unusual change of course. The girls snuck along behind the robot and dived into another booth.

'I can't stay long. Sabrina and Emma need me to shoot for their Instagrams, I've got to change into my beach outfit for this afternoon and my make-up is all over the place. I can't contour when I'm stressed.'

Jamie looked back at Daisy in surprise. Maybe Jenners was right. Daisy was cooler than the rest of them and that definitely didn't sound like an invite for the three of them to join.

'You're wearing make-up?' Jamie asked, slightly nervously.

'Yes, so what? When you're in Class 500K+ you need to actually make an effort,' said Daisy, which wasn't supposed to sound curt, but 100 per cent definitely did.

'Oh . . . OK.' Jamie felt like she was being told off for reasons she didn't fully understand.

'We were just saying, do you not think this place is weird? None of our parents want to FaceTime, me and Jenners have to eat spaghetti with our hands . . .'

'UGH, no, not really. It's creator school, Jamie – we don't need Mummy ringing us every day. TobyIsSoCoolLike said your year group is **underperforming** anyway. Maybe if you put some time into posting good content, you would get good meals at the canteen; it's not that hard.'

Daisy grabbed Mel's arm. 'Come on, Mel, Sabrina and Emma want you to be in the photo. Lunchtime is the second best time to post.'

'Yeah, yeah, go and run off to Sabrina Gumballs,' said Jamie, who had finally lost patience with Daisy. 'You go and run after some likes and hang around with horrible people while me and Jenners try to stay sane.'

'Jamie! If you just made the content, you'd get

more followers and then move into a better class! Why do you always have to be so **"Oooh, I'm going to do things Jamie McFlair's way and nobody else's"?** What did you think was going to happen at this school?'

'I thought we would get to still hang out together, instead of choosing our friends by how many followers they've got,' said Jamie, her voice **RISING.**

'You sure you're not just jealous because Mel has more followers than you?' said Daisy.

Jenners held up a hand.

'Hey, that's a foul, Daisy. That's a red card offence,' she said sternly.

'Am I wrong, though?' said Daisy.

Jamie was enraged. 'I don't care about followers!' she said, her voice rising. 'But I can see why you do, though. Carry on hiding behind big numbers and using silly berets to make up for your **lack of any real personality.'**

Everyone's faces fell.

There was a long awkward pause as Jamie suddenly realised she'd gone way too far. Jenners held up her hand again.

'Think that might be a **red card** for you, Jamie,' said Jenners.

'Come on, Mel, let's get out of here. Jamie McFlair being classic Jamie McFlair. You hate to see it,' said Daisy, shaking her head.

'Er, well . . . yeah, I suppose . . . bye, then,' mumbled Mel. Daisy marched out of the library, pulling Mel so harshly she almost tripped over her own feet.

There was an awkward silence between Jamie and Jenners.

'I'm not sure where all that came from. I was just so mad,' said Jamie, her cheeks glowing hot with **EMBARRASSMENT.**

'Yeah, I get the bit about the berets but the rest of it was way too far,' said Jenners, still clutching the paper pick'n'mix bag. 'Daisy was in the wrong too, though. This school has turned her into a right little . . .'

'Grotsack,' finished Jamie, which was probably good because Jenners was about to say a word not fit for books. 'I know I'm right about the school, though, it's a feeling I've had before. It's like my brain is screaming **"PANIC"** at me but I don't know why,' she went on.

'Brains are weird, though,' replied Jenners, trying to instil some library calm. 'My brain does the same thing when I see fruit. Besides, if by "last time" you mean when your mad uncle made literal monsters, that is different. There's no monsters here, unless you count homework content, which to be fair, does give me weird nightmares.'

'I know, I know . . .' But Jenners's words sparked more brain stress. *Something about this place reminds me of Barry . . . But that's just dumb . . . surely?* She considered saying something to Jenners, but dismissed it. She was being paranoid.

'RULE 347.5B.'

Jamie jumped in shock at the robot that had snuck up on them.

'YOU ARE BREACHING ONE PERSON PER BOOTH IN LOCATION ... LIBRARY. ALERTING FACULTY IN FIVE ... FOUR ...'

'I could definitely just **push it over,**' said Jenners, staring at the robot's ironically happy little face.

'I don't know, there's a rumour that they shoot sleeping darts and capture students in balls and make them battle each other ...' said Jamie.

'Sounds like fake news. And we have had a tough week,' said Jenners.

'Agreed. Get it,' said Jamie, and together they pushed the robot over with a large crash.

CHAPTER 18
CREATOR BURN-OUT

'Why couldn't we have built stairs?' muttered Slottapuss as he was slowly being raised by a winch. It was the only way to access Barry's office in the top tower of the Barry Castle. Slottapuss was attached to the thick cable by a harness. From the cable sprouted two large, **FEATHERED WINGS.** Slottapuss's long arms, legs and muzzle sagged and dangled sadly as he ascended, looking like he was about to be placed on top of the Christmas tree of an oddball.

At the top, Slottapuss, still wearing his shades and a snappy navy suit, wobbled on to the platform, gave the office door a knock and let himself in.

'Barry, we've got a situation—'

Barry held his hand up to silence his **RODENT HENCHMAN** and pointed to the plasma screen that hung above Barry's polar bear throne. Al G Rhythm was giving a school announcement.

Barry was sitting on the **THRONE,** holding a microphone and wearing a strange helmet. He also had little white dots all over his face. As he spoke, the big avatar of Al G Rhythm moved with Barry like a really high-tech lip sync. **'And remember, our biggest growers will face off in our boxing MAIN EVENT!** Keep up that growth! Holla holla, I've been Al G Rhythm and I approve this message.'

Barry tapped the touch screen, ending his broadcast, and started removing the motion-capture gear from his face.

'Impressive stuff, isn't it, Slotty? I'm so pleased that I'm not even going to berate you for interrupting my headmasteral broadcast. Turn that frown upside down, my **grotesque** friend. Why are you here?'

'Well, the initial reports from our school analytics department are in,' Slottapuss said, nervously pulling out some documents that were hard to read because the printer was running out of ink. 'They monitor how close we are to our school target of one billion followers.'

Once Barry had removed his helmet, he also removed his polar bear coat and dropped his trousers.

'Um . . . So . . . yeah, anyway . . .' Slottapuss stammered, trying to pretend everything was normal. 'Student followings aren't growing as fast as we would like. We currently have a combined student total of **fifty five million followers,** which is . . . less than a billion . . .'

Barry, who was now only wearing a disturbingly small pair of lilac Speedos, skipped over to his office Jacuzzi and turned on the roaring bubbles before clambering inside.

'So . . . I know we are aiming for the **Ultimate Brain Hack** to take place during the big boxing match,' said Slottapuss, who now had to raise his voice over the rumble of the bubbles, 'but based on this current trajectory, it's going to take a while longer for the students to have enough followers for **Operation Ultimate Brain Hack.**'

'How long's a while?' said Barry, who was now sucking on a glass of Choco Moo Juice.

'Give or take, at this current speed, we'd be ready in . . . around two hundred and sixty-seven years,' said Slottapuss.

BARRY SPAT OUT HIS MOO JUICE, which made it look like someone had committed a bottom crime in the Jacuzzi.

'Slotty. Can't you see I'm in a Jacuzzi?'

The rodent-man nodded.

'I'm trying to relax. That is not relaxing information.'

'What should we do?' asked Slottapuss.

'Speed things up, obviously!' said Barry, sploshing impatiently. 'Increase the demand for new pieces of content this week from **ten to twenty**. Then next week we bump that up from twenty to forty, make the teachers teach them better. Whatever it takes to get those little weasel internet fans to follow them. Maybe we just steal their brains as soon as the machine is ready. Especially if my snot-nosed germ of a niece is under our control . . . Ask StompyBlob what is taking him so long as well! Can't he just give her some of his followers? Also, start cutting privileges of those kids that are seeing their numbers dwindle. That should encourage them to **try harder,'** Barry ranted, sploshing at the end of every sentence.

Slottapuss nodded. 'OK . . . Should also add that . . . our students are a bit stressed with things as they are . . . Couple of our Class 250–500Ks had a breakdown in YouTube Drama. Think realities got a bit blurred there . . . A lot of our students are saying outrageous things they don't mean just to boost their numbers . . . One kid has got a **permanently shocked** thumbnail face . . . There's been a couple of attacks on the robots . . . A lot of our students seem a bit sad and that might be down to the current growth demands.'

Barry's mouth hung open and there was silence other than the hum of the Jacuzzi.

'Slotty. Are you dumb? I know we're running a school but we're not **ACTUALLY** running a school here. That's not the point of any of this. Stop calling them OUR students. They're not our students – this is a content farm and they're our livestock. We don't **CARE** about their wellbeing. We don't **CARE** about their learning experience. We're all here to get their cretinous little brains under MY control, then use their millions of followers to spread the word of my innocence. That's the game. I don't care how loopy it sends them. If they complain, just fill their rooms with more stuff! Lay on some more disco parties. Use your vile and manipulative skills to make sure we'll be ready to get these chickens laying view-filled eggs. **That clear?'**

Slottapuss nodded.

'You're not going soft on me, are you, Slotty? You were starting to sound like that stupid bear just then,' said Barry, sinking into the bubbles.

'No, sir,' said Slottapuss as he left the office, thinking about some of the fun times he used to have with Henrik. He looked at his phone calendar.

- Write more fake student messages from parents
- Write more fake student messages to parents
- Increase Ultimate Brain Hack headset production
- Garbage bath

Slottapuss was about to disappear down the slide when a cry came from the hot tub.

'Slot-Slots! I've just had an idea,' said Barry.

'Yes, boss?' the rat replied.

'Can you make our next experiment one of Jamie McFlair's little chums?' said Barry, making cruel mini sploshes. 'Since she seems to care about her friends so much. Maybe that will get her to work a **little harder.**'

'Will get that sorted now, boss,' said Slottapuss as he disappeared down the slide.

CHAPTER 19

INTRUSION OF GARBAGE PRIVACY

Jamie remembered when making TikToks was fun. It felt like a distant lifetime ago that she, Jenners, Mel and Daisy would perfect their own **BNA-themed dance routines.** Making fifteen TikToks a day, however, was not fun. Jamie had hardly seen Mel, and Daisy hadn't replied to a single message in the group chat since the library.

'Looks like we might be seeing the first member of our tutor group take the big step up to the class above!' said StompyDog to the tutor group. **'Congratulations, JENNERS!'**

Jenners had her head in her hands. Despite her best efforts to the contrary, her videos just seemed to do better and better. The Prince Alfred Dribblewater videos she'd made in the first few weeks had exploded.

Jenners had even completely stopped making content but because her numbers were skyrocketing, nobody told her off and it was completely out of her control.

The class clapped and Jenners shrugged.

'Jamie, dude. Quick word before you go to Show and Tell,' said Stompy.

The rest of the class waded out of the room through the ball pit.

'Hey, Jamie, you really need to step up the followers, dude!' said Stompy. 'I know you think a lot of it is silly, but surely you don't want to be left in your class on your own? Hey, cos I'm a pal and to give you a boost, I'll duet with you on your next TikTok assignment. **How does that sound?** Hopefully that should keep you and Jenners together?'

Jamie, who was still a year away from learning the word 'ambivalence', was feeling it in very strong doses here. In case you've forgotten, it's a word that means feeling two opposite emotions about the same thing. *A duet with StompyDog! Being asked personally! Staying with Jenners in the new class! Awesome!* But the Barry

thoughts wouldn't go away. Maybe
she could confide in Stompy? *Maybe I could ask
for his help at the duet.*

She thanked StompyDog and caught up with Jenners
in the corridor.

'A duet!? With actual StompyDog?' Jenners yelled
on max volume. 'Maybe things are looking up!'

'*PSSSSHHHHHHHHH* . . . This is a school
announcement,' came the booming voice from the
tannoy for the second time already that morning.
'Please be aware that your requirements have now
been increased to fifty pieces of content per day, which
is great news and you will see your follower numbers
SKYROCKET! Get out there and **CRUSH IT!**'

'OK, maybe not,' said Jamie.

'FIFTY!? Stupid Al G Rhythm and his mischievous
eyebrows,' said Jenners as they made their way to
Show and Tell, which was like normal show and tell
but you were only allowed to bring in products you'd
been sponsored by.

Jamie's list of weird occurrences at Rubbslings

School for Creators and Influencers now nearly filled the entire BNA notepad. Every day there was something new to add and, worst of all, her mum seemed to be ignoring her concerns and Scott had completely ignored her message. So much for owing her one. Jamie was starting to **HATE** Rubbslings School. She hated the lessons, the constant homework and after the Daisy incident she'd even started to hate herself. *Maybe I've also been too harsh on Daisy. Maybe she had a point and I should just get more followers?* She felt like the school was turning her into a horrible person. She typed a message to Mel.

Jamie

Hey Mel, can you please tell Daisy I am super sorry. I dont think she is reading my messages :(:(tell her that I hate that I said that she had no personality. Everyone loves her and i was just jealous that u were enjoying school way more than me, i feel so bad. :(:(:(

Send.
Mel is typing . . .

Mel

Hey I would but haven't seen her since Monday and neither has Sabrina?

Jamie felt a **PANG OF GUILT** in her stomach. All she had wanted was her friends to stick together and she'd been the one to cause the arguments. Her brain started to run away with unhelpful thoughts, in the way that brains do sometimes.

What if I am the one who forced everyone apart? Maybe if we'd have gone to different schools, none of this would've happened. Why do we have less people in our class? Where are they? Where's Daisy?

'Do you know or not?' said Jenners, a little too sternly for friends.

'Know what?' asked Jamie.

'What room we're supposed to go to – is it **Crying Emoji Room or Laughing Emoji Room?** They look the same! I've asked you like three times!' said Jenners, while herself making a confused emoji face.

'Sorry . . . sorry . . . I can't stop thinking about this stupid school, it's driving me mad,' said Jamie, raising her voice over the clattering of the other students sprinting to lessons. 'Let's get Show and Tell done and then go to the beach. Also, most of Daisy's content is made at the beach. If she's anywhere, that's where she'll be. **I'll tell Mel to meet us there.** Maybe the school has finally gotten to Daisy, too; she might have just taken a mini holiday.'

'I think everyone could do with one, to be honest . . .' said Jenners as they paused to observe the bedlam around them. Creators and influencers were darting around like pixies at a disco, desperately trying to make as much content as they could.

'And remember, if you **LOVE THIS VIDEO,** smash that Like button . . . **LIKE AND SUBSCRIBE, GUYS** . . . **SUBSCRIBE TO MY PATREON** . . . Remember to **GET THAT MERCH** . . .'

'Please, I'm sorry to interrupt, do you have any food, a snack, a high-caffeine drink, a sugary sweet, anything? I'll swap you it for any of these games.'

Standing in front of the girls was a boy who could only have been six or seven years old, looking **DESPERATE** and clutching an armful of computer games.

'Erm . . . yeah, OK, I might have a snack bar, hang on . . . Are you all right?' Jenners replied, trying to squash her annoyance of having to potentially give up a snack bar.

'I haven't had breakfast . . . or dinner last night. I'm losing subscribers and I can't get in the canteen any more. They keep giving me games for my videos but I can't eat these,' said the boy, who seemed far too young to be roaming around school on his own.

'They won't let you in? But you've got to eat!' said Jamie with genuine annoyance. 'That's mad . . . Here you go, of course.' She grabbed Jenners's snack bar and a box of raisins and handed them over.

'Oh thank you, thank you, thank you,' replied the boy as he snatched them out of her hand, looked both ways and immediately sprinted down the hall.

'This is getting ridiculous,' said Jenners. 'This is the fourth snack bar I've had to give away to a starving kid this week. **Everyone's nuts.'**

Once the class was over, Jamie and Jenners once again battled through what is probably best described as absolute, complete **MADNESS-BASED CHAOS.** Everywhere they looked, it seemed like people were either unbelievably stressed or overly energetic, filming videos. The girls peered into the Class 0–10K common room, which they never spent much time in because it was always the least relaxing place ever.

At least seven other influencers lay motionless, face-down on top of a ball pit, even as a boy with a **GOPRO ON HIS HEAD** was visibly shaking a vending machine next to them in rage. Someone next to him was wearing a VR headset and seemed to be boxing a cardboard cut-out of himself.

They picked up their pace and headed down to the
Rubbslings School iron gates, where they met Mel and
set off in the direction of the beach. The wind was
blowing and it was starting to rain, two things that
shouldn't go along with **NICE BEACH TIMES.**

'DAISY!' bellowed Jenners at a volume that Daisy
could probably hear on a trip to the moon.

'DAISY, IT'S JUST US, WE'RE NOT HERE TO MAKE CONTENT!' shouted Jamie.

The girls split up to search the entire beach at the front of the island, down by the scanners and back up around the main school building, but Jamie could see no trace of her friend.

'No sign of Daisy,' said Mel, as they came back together. 'I thought I'd found the goose for a second but it was someone's **blue robot parrot.'**

'Let's explore the rest of the school,' said Jamie as they headed towards the bizarre buildings of the island.

'Could she be in there?' Jenners said, pointing to the hulking monstrosity of the island's castle.

'We aren't allowed in,' said Jamie, rattling on the front door. 'For graduates and teachers, apparently. **Let's look around.'**

Around the side of the castle were old boxes and the bins, but what they saw next made them stop in their tracks. Hanging out the side of one of the dumpsters was a long strand of blonde hair.

'DAISY!' the girls yelled.

Jenners heaved open the dumpster.

'False alarm. It's a fabulous wig,' she said, before tossing it on to Mel's head.

'Eew, bin wig, gross,' said Mel.

'Hey, there's loads of weird stuff in here,' said Jenners. 'Oh my—'

'What?' said Jamie.

'Jamie. Think you'll want to take a look at this,' she said, in the style of a TV detective that she'd stayed up past her bedtime to watch.

'Oh my . . . What on earth?' said Jamie, peering into the dumpster. 'What are these, like gross old statues?' she said, climbing up and reaching inside to pull one out.

Soggy from rain and bin juice, Jamie held up an ugly-looking papier-mâché bust, like one of those ancient Greek head-and-shoulder statues you see in textbooks. The statue wasn't of an ancient Greek person, though – it was of someone else. Someone who all of the girls recognised.

'Is that . . . Is that supposed to be **Barry Bigtime?'** said Jamie and dropped it suddenly with a squelch.

Jenners dove into the dumpster, while Mel nervously stood guard. She'd vowed never to look in a dumpster again after the last time she'd gone looking for garbage clues.

'There's loads of them!' said Jenners, tossing more and more soggy papier-mâché Barry busts out into the daylight.

Just the sight of the weird sculptures was causing Jamie's heart to beat faster and her breath to quicken. The dumpster was full of them. It was like seeing mouldy bread or maggots in the bin. Her brain hadn't even really had time to work out what was going on, but she knew that this was wrong.

'Why do you think these are here?' asked Jenners.

'I uh . . . for . . . content, I don't know?' said Jamie, her voice shaking.

'I reckon we rip it open. There might be treasure or

clues hidden inside!' said Jenners. 'Actually, wait, what if it's poison gases?' She shook the statue, listening closely for any rattle, but it was too squelchy to tell. 'Might just punch it anyway,' said Jenners, who immediately squashed the Barry face with **A BIG FIST.**

'Errrr, guys . . . I think we might have company,' said Mel, who suddenly felt like being inside the dumpster might be the safest place to be.

The girls had been so absorbed by the Barry sculptures they hadn't noticed one of the school patrol robots approaching.

'RULE 415.5B – YOU ARE BREACHING INTRUSION OF GARBAGE PRIVACY. LOCATION: CASTLE. RELEASING TRANQUILLISERS IN FIVE . . . FOUR . . .

'RUN!' said Jenners and sprinted back to the accommodation with the Barry bust under her arm.

CHAPTER 20
THE CLIFFSIDE CAMP

Proudy opened the trash bag to find a dazed, gunged girl wearing a beret.

Be honest, how many girls do you know that wear berets? Out of those girls, how many can make it look good while being in a garbage bag? Sorry but yes, it's the girl you think it is. **WE WISH IT WASN'T, TOO.**

'Another one?' he asked.

'Think this one might be the final one,' said Flobster, removing a pair of oven gloves he used to stop his deep-sea snippers from compromising the integrity of the refuse sack.

'Barry thinks he's got the formula right this time. How are the others doing?'

There was an awkward silence as Proudy paused. The silence was broken as a boy with a microwave for a head stumbled into view.

'Some of the experimented-on kids are doing better than others, Flobster, I'll be honest,' said Proudy, who was an optimistic fellow.

'What happened to him?' asked Flobster.

'He just won't take his head out of that microwave. Otherwise he's completely normal,' said Proudy. 'Hey, Microwave Kid, come over here,' he yelled. The kid stumbled over and Proudy pressed the button to swing the door open, revealing a friendly face inside.

'Hey, Proudy!' said Microwave Kid cheerfully. 'Aaarrghh! Oh my goodness, what is that?!' He **SCREAMED** on sight of Flobster and slammed his microwave door shut.

'See, other than that he's totally normal,' said Proudy with a shrug.

'Barry has requested that any defective students become **shark food.** Please add it to your list,' snapped Flobster. 'We can't take any more from the school; time is ticking and McFlair is sticking her nose in again. It's making Mr Bigtime . . . irritable . . . and gassy.'

'Sounds like irritable bowel syndrome. My doctor says that stress—' Proudy was interrupted by the latest experiment poking her head out of the bag.

'Where am I?' said Daisy as she tried to climb out of her bin bag.

'Keep an eye on this one, she's a wriggly little customer,' said Flobster. 'And she was one of the ones who helped orchestrate the whole fuss at the World Music Festival. Barry will be very keen to **control her brain,** so claws crossed for no signs of defects.'

'Yeah, hope so!' said Proudy cheerfully. 'As it's getting a bit mad up here. We're starting to run out of space . . . Come on, buddy, up you get!' he said as he helped Daisy to her feet. He put an arm round her and took her to camp.

Barry had left his old boybands on the island to start initial preparations for his plan many, many months ago. He hadn't left them with any real supplies, though, so they had essentially formed their own tribe to survive and built the **CLIFFSIDE CAMP.** Some of the boys had gone all in, complete with tribal dress.

(See, we told you we'd eventually explain Proudy's loincloth thing.)

Proudy had had a weird life. He was very pure and innocent at heart. He was only fifteen when he went in the Boyband Generator eleven years ago. He was part of Baezone, the **JEWEL IN BARRY'S BOYBAND CROWN.** They had enjoyed all of the lovely things that come with such a title. World tours, screaming crowds, luxurious living. Then as quickly as it started, the fame had vanished, which made him sad. Last October, Proudy and the band went to Barry's big party hoping that he could kick-start their career again. Instead, Barry ended up stealing their talents . . . Yet despite all this, Proudy still hoped that one day Barry Bigtime would come up with a plan for Baezone that would bring all their nice times back. Why else would he be on a deserted island in a loincloth?

The little **TRIBAL BOYBAND VILLAGE** was bustling with absurd scenes. Wigwams were dotted around the edge of the camp and in the middle was a large totem pole. Carved in each segment were the logos of Baezone, The Fenton Dogz, Kouros and The Lord North Lads. Boyband members of the past bustled around busily in **FURS AND LOINCLOTHS,** either completing camp tasks or assisting the other student experiments. Some students looked like their brains were being controlled by a child pressing all the buttons on a keyboard at the same time. One boy in particular, dressed as a chef, was dancing an Irish jig while mooing. Another had his head buried deep into the sand and another one seemed to be continuously bowing to nobody in particular.

'So what's your name, buddy?' asked Proudy.

'Daisy?' said Daisy, not looking totally sure. 'Uh . . . how did I get here . . . Why am I gross?'

Proudy absolutely hated lying and left this job to the tribal truth-twister Francois, who was waiting for them by the totem pole.

'Francois here tells me you won a contest, isn't that right, Francois?'

'That is right!' said Francois with

his silky French accent. 'Your numbers grew so much that you won a two-week holiday on the Cliffside Camp!'

'Oh yeah, I remember . . .' said Daisy with a glazed look in her eyes.

'And the celebrations were so wild you fell in the **gunge of triumph!'** insisted Francois.

'Oh, yeah, that makes sense,' said Daisy.

Proudy and Francois exchanged a thumbs up. This one did look promising. At least she wasn't barking like a dog.

'Here's your holiday tent!' said Proudy, proudly.

'I'll just get settled, shall I?' said Daisy, who looked completely unbothered by the situation. Proudy gave another thumbs up.

'If you need anything, buddy, give me a shout!' said Proudy as she crawled happily into her new wigwam home.

'Hey, Proudy, do you think if this kid really lasts the two weeks with no defects, and it means the Ultimate Brain Hack works and Barry does his plan thing, then we can all go back to making music? Travelling the road? **Maybe even go home?'** said Francois.

'I hope so, man. Barry promised that if we stuck this out, then he'd make us stars again,' said Proudy. He crossed his fingers. Daisy was their best chance yet.

Inside her tent, Daisy was having a very confusing time and not just because she was sticky with gunge. She'd felt like there had been two Daisys in her head since she arrived at the school. One that begged her to be with Jamie, Jenners and Mel and one that wanted to have big numbers after her name and be liked by Sabrina Gumbear and the other Class 500K+s. Talia had been filling her head with promises of fame and fortune and cool points all summer. **'Keep the right company'** and **'Post the right things'**, she kept saying.

However, for the first time since she stepped foot on the Rubbslings sand, those voices seemed to have disappeared. Now there was one strange, new voice. One voice that made her think about what had happened at the World Music Festival. She could see, clear in her mind, the monsters wreaking havoc. The voice made her feel like it was all her fault. If she hadn't gone along with the plan, there would have been no monster. And what had happened? Poor Barry Bigtime got the blame. He hadn't even realised he'd made the monster. And now he'd lost everything. She'd helped take an innocent man's house and dreams. How could she do such a thing! She felt so bad about it she thought she was going to cry. **SHE PICKED UP HER PHONE.**

New Vlog: Title: Why I was wrong about Barry Bigtime.

CHAPTER 21
JAMIE'S FAVOURITE FILTER

The girls had sprinted back to their rooms after managing to shake the robot.

'This has gone far enough,' said Jamie to herself as she started tearing the pages of findings from her notepad.

I need to find all the old episodes of The Big Time *that I can, study old Barry Bigtime websites, the spy-man glasses footage from last year and cross-reference it with some of the strange things I've written in my notepad.* Jamie desperately didn't want her hunches to be right. She hoped with all her might that there was an innocent reason for what they'd found in the dumpster. But she needed to be sure. **SHE HAD WORK TO DO.**

The next day after lessons, Jamie went to find Mel

and Jenners and brought them back to her room, passing the after-school mayhem of creators who were now desperately trying to create sixty pieces of panic-content a day.

Just as she went to touch her phone on the access panel, Jamie paused.

'I didn't tell you yet because I wasn't sure, **but now I am,**' she said as her bedroom door slid across.

Jenners made a face that could be used as a shocked reaction GIF for years to come.

'What . . . on . . .' said Mel, looking around. Jamie's room looked a bit like her old *old* room that she used to share with Grandma. It was covered with pieces of paper, but instead of BNA posters, they were filled with **MAD SCRIBBLES.**

'Jamie, this is mad. I'm here for it, but also can you just let me know if you've lost your mind or not? Like no judgement, just be good for me to know,' said Jenners.

'I think for the first time since Nica Konstantopolous's shoe launch, I'm thinking clearly,'

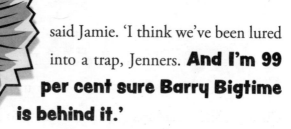

said Jamie. 'I think we've been lured into a trap, Jenners. **And I'm 99 per cent sure Barry Bigtime is behind it.**'

Mel looked like she was going to need some convincing and potentially some oxygen.

'I've noted down all the weird stuff I could remember over the last few weeks, and started properly investigating, looking for any patterns in the weirdness. And look at all this . . . How did we find out about this school?' asked Jamie.

The girls took a pause. 'At Nica's event?' Mel replied.

'Yes. We got stopped by that **Billy Clarkson** man. So I did some digging on this Billy Clarkson character and his connection to Nica Konstantopolous. All I could find is from this old showbiz blog by someone called The Pop Prince. All about how Nica's bandmate ended up in space at Billy Clarkson's sixtieth birthday party. And where was the birthday party held? At Uncle Barry's mansion.'

Jenners and Mel raised an eyebrow.

'And that's not all,' Jamie continued. 'I downloaded the footage of the spy-man glasses from last year for clues.' She handed her tablet to Jenners. 'Look! There is the purple dinosaur that threw me in the dumpster at the boyband party. Now, when did we see that purple dinosaur again? On the boat to the school. He gave Jenners the lollies!'

Jenners and Mel **RAISED A FURTHER EYEBROW.**

'Also, the golf carts here . . .' she said, pointing at a drawing of the ones from the school. 'I examined them yesterday lunchtime, and they are all Albatross500s. Cross-reference that with the two my mum had to put up on eBay last year when clearing out Uncle Barry's old stuff and look, Albatross500s.'

Jenners and Mel had no more eyebrows to raise so opened their mouths to express surprise.

'Also, in the corridor heading into the canteen, the "Stuff = Happiness" poster. We had a weird tapestry with that exact phrase at the mansion. Me and Grandma ripped it up and used it for dusters because it was so cringe.'

Jenners and Mel gasped.

'Then there's the weird statue things we just found. We know **Barry loves a statue of himself.** Remember how many we had to get rid of from my garden? I bet he had those made, then thought they were either too ugly or too obvious and had them binned.'

Jenners and Mel gasped, but a bit louder this time.

'AND the boys who greeted us on the first day at the beach. I couldn't place it at the time – it's just **Sawyer from The Fenton Dogz** with different hair! And we all know The Fenton Dogz were one of the boybands that disappeared with Barry after the World Music Festival.'

Jenners and Mel gasped louder still.

'I also found this on an archived page from a thing called Bebo.'

'Wait, what on earth is that?' asked Jenners.

'Dunno, but Henrik had an account on there in 2005 and uploaded four pictures. It's one of him working in a theme park for Uncle Barry, and look. **Recognise that castle?'**

Jenners and Mel did their loudest gasp yet.

Jamie took a deep breath. 'AND finally. If you're still not convinced, look at this.'

Jamie opened up two videos side by side on her tablet. One was of the headmaster Al G Rhythm; the other was a video entitled 'Barry Bigtime's WORST audition ROASTS'.

'Look at the eyebrows . . .'

Those four eyebrows were so in sync they could start their own TikTok dance troupe.

Jenners gave a yelp and immediately covered her hands with her mouth. Mel was hitting two gasps per second and needed to immediately lie down.

'Add that to Percival and Javed disappearing, the weird messages from our parents, suspicious emoji use and everything else . . . What do you guys think?'

'Jamie, I think we can upgrade that 99 per cent hunch to a full **100 per cent hunch,'** said Jenners.

Jamie looked more sad than triumphant. 'I'm so sorry for leading us into a trap; I thought we were going to be safe. **I've been so stupid!'**

'Nah, we were all up for the school, Jamie. I didn't want to go to stupid Strumptons. Mel didn't want to get her head flushed down the toilet. If anyone should be sorry, it's our parents for being dumb enough to let us come to a mad internet school, to be honest,' said Jenners. 'This is going to be a hard sell for Daisy, though . . .' she added.

'We need to message Daisy and tell her!' Mel said from the floor. 'She'll reply if she knows that she might be in danger!'

'I've tried!' said Jamie. 'She won't even read my messages; it's like she's **blocked my number** or just doesn't want to know any more.'

'She doesn't reply to the group ones either,' added Jenners, which everybody already knew but nobody wanted to admit. 'What do we do?'

'I've got an idea!' said Mel. She

pulled out her phone and started scrolling through old posts like a maniac.

'FOUND IT!' She showed the photo to Jamie.

The photo was one of Jamie sitting in her bedroom, pouting and holding up four fingers to camera, with no caption, just a Valencia filter and one hashtag: #FourThirty. Jamie's eyes widened. This pose was what Jamie, Jenners, Mel and Daisy called the **VALENCIAN FOUR-FINGERED SALUTE.** A lot had happened since they had last used it, but its meaning would never be forgotten. The Valencian Four-Fingered Salute was the girls' secret sign when an emergency group gathering needed to be called. It was decided upon because it could be used from anywhere. If their phones had been confiscated and the group chat was out of action, they could log in from a computer or borrow a mate's phone and still post. **THEY AND ONLY THEY KNEW WHAT IT MEANT.**

Jamie immediately grabbed her two friends, pulling on their jumpers to get them in shot. The three girls pouted and raised four fingers into the air. Jamie slid across to add the Valencia filter and then paused.

She glanced at the time – 3.57 p.m. – and typed **#FOURTHIRTY** to signify the time that the meeting would be held, followed by **#ROOM32B.**

She was about to post when Jenners grabbed the phone.

OMG!! Nica Konstantopolous's new shoes are unbelievable, 😍 love, love, LOVE THEM! 😍 👠 🖤

she wrote, and hit 'post'.

By now you know Jamie pretty well and you know that this is not the kind of caption she would be posting on any normal day. If you've worked out why Nica Konstantopolous's shoes are mentioned in it, you should consider signing up to be a detective **IMMEDIATELY.**

'If she doesn't reply to this, something is definitely up,' said Jamie nervously. *Please, Daisy, like this post,* Jamie thought.

Jenners likes this.

Mel likes this.

Plumsquash and 35 others like this.

And the comments started flooding in.

Oh my days, didn't know you loved her range.

I've always wanted a pair of her shoes, spenny though!

Nothing from Daisy.

The next thirty-three minutes took for ever, as the girls sat through and listened to BNA's entire first album. They barely said a word but instead sat refreshing the comments, hoping for a response from Daisy.

'She's not coming,' said Jamie, breaking the silence. 'I'm really worri—'

'She's posted!' said Mel excitedly.

There on Daisy's feed was Daisy herself, looking normal other than her beret was askew and make-up not quite on point to her usual standard.

Mel turned the volume up on her phone and scrolled down slightly to the caption.

'Why I was wrong about Barry Bigtime', read the title.

'What the . . .' were the only words that Jenners managed to produce.

'I feel sick,' said Jamie, who grabbed her friends' arms, bracing herself for what was to come.

'Hello, my name is Daisy Palmer. You might recognise me as one of the girls who once helped take down Barry Bigtime, who lots of people thought was a bad man. Well, unfortunately, a lot of what was in the news was wrong about him . . .'

The girls watched in **DISBELIEF.** They wanted to peel their eyes away from the screen but sat motionless.

'It's not her,' said Jamie.

'That is definitely Daisy,' replied Jenners. 'Look at it!'

'Yes, I mean it's not *her* – it's not the Daisy we know. She would never in a million years do that video herself. Something's wrong,' Jamie said, taking control.

'But what do we do!?' asked Mel. 'If we post about it and they have got her, they'll come for us as well.'

'We act like nothing has happened,' said Jamie.

'What??' Jenners raised her voice. 'That's Daisy! She might have got a bit big for her boots but **she's still our friend.'**

'I know, I know . . .' reassured Jamie, 'but she's only just posted it. We pretend we haven't seen it.'

'Is there anyone on this island we can trust?' asked Jenners.

'What about StompyDog?' asked Jamie.

Mel chimed in, 'But he's a teacher; how do we know that all the teachers aren't on Team Barry?'

'Well, put it this way: if we can trust him, he'll be able to help. If we can't, he knows where Daisy is, so we make him talk,' said Jamie as she grabbed her slime blaster and loaded in the cartridges.

CHAPTER 22
UNDERCOVER STOMPYDOG

Mr StompyDog's door was open but for once the girls disobeyed the knocking first policy and barged right in.

'Woahh, yo, McFlair, Jenners and if I'm not mistaken, top of the school, Mel, isn't it?'

Mel nodded and smiled, then immediately remembered why they were there.

'Aren't you all finished for the day? **How can I help?**' said the smiley, sing-song Stompy.

'Can you take us to the headmaster, please, Mr StompyDog? We would like to speak to him,' said Jamie, probably too sternly for teachers.

Mr StompyDog's eyes **NARROWED.** 'Hey, look, Mr Rhythm is very busy, y'know.'

'This is important.' said Jenners. She was about the same height as Mr StompyDog. Her fists were clenching.

'Why can't we see him? Why have none of us ever met him? Who is he?' said Jamie as she reached into her backpack and placed one hand on the **SLIME BLASTER.**

'I'll put it this way: he's a very smart, very unpredictable person who doesn't like surprise visits. You'd be wise to stop asking questions and return to your dormitories, please, girls.'

'Why can't we see him? Are you afraid of him?' said Jenners, leaning in and on the precipice of becoming **JENZILLA.**

'I've been doing some . . . extracurricular research that I think you might want to see,' Jamie replied. She pulled the loose pages of evidence from her bag and spread them on the table in front of him. 'Something **strange is going on** and I think I know who is behind it.'

Mr StompyDog's eyes darted over the pages. A little trickle of sweat rolled down his forehead.

'Right, I need to ask you girls to

stop being dumb for a second,' said StompyDog in a tone the girls hadn't heard him use before.

'What do you know, Stompy? You have to tell us. Is my uncle **– Barry Bigtime –** is he secretly running the school—'

'First off, I don't need to tell any of you anything. You got that?' said StompyDog, raising his voice. 'And you need to shut right up about Barry Bigtime if you know what's good for you.'

Jenners and Mel were stunned, but Jamie was defiant. **'Why?'**

'You girls aren't safe here,' he whispered in a hushed tone.

'We know, that's why we want to find our friend and leave,' said Jamie.

'No, but you *can't* leave. They won't let you leave . . .' StompyDog closed his eyes. 'Barry Bigtime won't let you leave.'

Jamie's mouth fell open. She couldn't believe it. Their own tutor and childhood hero knew all along? And didn't help them?

'You . . . knew?' said Jamie.

'Right, I want you to listen to me, real good, OK, girls. This is for all of our sakes – we're all in a heck lot of danger. So I've not necessarily been . . . who you think I am,' said Stompy under his breath.

'Yeah, you've been playing nice with us knowing Barry Bigtime is luring us into a trap!' said Jenners angrily.

'No, that's not what it is at all. I'm working **undercover** under the instructions of Detective Lansdown. Which you didn't know about and still don't know about.' Stompy stared intently at the girls, checking they understood. 'Barry is a high-risk wanted man, as you know. Eight months ago, Detective Lansdown got intel that Barry had a new **top-secret** plan, potentially involving influencers. That's when they came to me. That's why I disappeared from YouTube. Barry knows you're here; in fact, he recruited you. This operation has to be done the right way so we don't spook him and we stop him ever doing something like this again.'

'Why wouldn't you get us in on this before?' said Jamie. 'We would do anything to help!'

'I didn't wanna put you girls in danger,' said Stompy. 'Thought I'd keep an eye on you, not that you need it. You three can handle yourselves for sure.'

'Has he got Daisy?' asked Mel, who didn't really want to ask the question or know the answer.

'I think so,' said Stompy, lowering his eyes. 'I

think he's got a few of the students who have gone missing. Have you seen her post?'

The girls nodded.

'What's he doing with them!? What's his plan?' asked Jamie.

'I don't know for sure but I think it's going ahead tomorrow evening.'

'At the boxing match . . . ?' said Jamie **'The whole school will be distracted!'**

'You've got it,' said Stompy. 'One step ahead of the game. You don't disappoint, Jamie McFlair. I have to stop him before the match.'

'Well, we're coming with you. We're stronger together. I know how he thinks. We're putting an end to all this,' Jamie said.

'He's a dangerous man, Jamie, you'd be far safer and better off—'

Jamie interrupted. 'We. Are. Coming. With. You. **Daisy needs us.'**

Stompy threw up his hands. 'Fine. Fine. To be

honest, I could use a few extra pairs of hands. You have to promise me that you keep quiet and don't do anything stupid before the boxing match, OK?'

'Promise. **PROMISE!! Pinky promise,'** the girls said.

'The boxing match is at 8.30 p.m., so we'll meet you where . . . ?' Jamie looked at Stompy.

'Eight p.m. Outside the castle. Tell no one,' he replied.

The three of them nodded. Jamie grabbed the loose papers with one hand and Mel's hand with the other and left without saying a word.

CHAPTER 23
HENRIK'S VERY OWN CHAPTER

Henrik raised his fist above the chopping board and then slammed it down, **PUMMELLING** the garlic clove. Whacking garlic with his bear paw really was an effective way to mince it and he'd become quite the chef of late. Not being an evil henchman these past few months had freed up a lot of time, which meant he could focus his energy on activities that he enjoyed far more and that also tasted much more delicious than **EVIL WRONGDOINGS.** He also liked to pay his way at the mansion by cooking dinner for Sarah and Dominic and had even bought himself a dedicated fez for the kitchen. Sous-chef Buttons the pug was hoovering the floor for scraps.

'One call, one call is all I'd like!' said Sarah from the kitchen table. 'Regular calls, **we agreed,** not one-

or-two-word emoji-based messages.' She held out her phone, showing a message from Jamie that said:

Great thanks! Loving Rubbslings!

'I hadn't even asked her a question!'

'Oh, she's probably having the time of her life. Kids will be kids! If she's having half the crazy time I had at school, she won't have time for her parents!' said Dominic cheerfully. This was also a lie – Dominic had not had a crazy time at school. He'd got excellent grades and no detentions, but still.

'Talk of the devil! Jamie's just posted here, look – aww, Jenners too. "*OMG!! Nica Konstantopolous's new shoes are unbelievable, heart eyes emoji, love, love, LOVE THEM! Heart eyes emoji, regular heart, shoe emoji*",' read Sarah, loudly enough so Henrik could hear.

Henrik's fist slipped, this time completely missing the garlic and catching the edge of the pan. It made a large sizzle sound as the hot pan frazzled Henrik's fur and burnt through to the skin. Henrik yelled in pain,

plunging his hand under the cold tap.

'Goodness, Henrik, are you OK, dear?' asked Sarah, concerned but not entirely shocked. 'That's it, keep it under that cold tap for a while.'

Henrik looked **EMBARRASSED.** With one hand under the tap, he reached over, placed an onion on the chopping board and began pummelling it even harder than the garlic.

Sarah continued, 'Yeah, I suppose she must be enjoying it, especially if she's buying shoes that may or may not have been designed by Nica Konstantopolous, my childhood idol.'

'FOR THE LOVE OF SALMON,' screeched Henrik as he accidentally slid his other paw straight on to the hot plate.

'Oh, Henrik, dear! Again? What's got into you?' This time Sarah leapt to her feet and grabbed two of the large jugs from the kitchen shelf. 'Here, let me fill these up with cold water and then come with me, sit down and hold both your paws in each one. That was clumsy even for you! Dominic, finish off dinner, will you?'

'Sorry. I don't know what happened,' said Henrik glumly. 'It's almost ready; you just need to make the onion jus.'

Henrik was used to being embarrassed so was not particularly bothered that he now had two temporarily unusable paws, but still something didn't sit right with him. His brain began to daydream as he sat helplessly with his paws in jugs. Henrik was a big bear but wasn't so tough on the inside. When he used to play Flower Samurais of Death with the girls, he was often the first one to get hurt and they'd have to briefly pause to check he was all right. That was probably part of the reason he was never a very good **EVIL HENCHMAN** for Barry. Henrik missed the girls; he missed playing games with them, carrying them on his back, misunderstanding their jokes. They'd always have to explain them to him, which made everyone laugh. '*If you ever see us being legitimately excited about Nica Konstantopolous shoes, you know we're in trouble . . .*'

'Do you think this jus suits the pink Himalayan salt or the regular sea salt?' interrupted Dominic.

Sarah rolled her eyes. 'I really don't think it matters, Dominic.'

'In which case, aubergine puttanesca with roasted spaghetti squash and a caramelised onion jus à la Chef Henrik is ready!' announced Dominic.

Henrik waddled over to the kitchen table, clinging on to the full jugs with his still sore paws. He sat himself down next to Dominic's laptop that had been kindly donated by Rubbslings School for Creators and Influencers. Even the screensaver was Rubbslings themed. 'Might have to eat this in a more traditional bear-like fashion, guys, if that's OK,' said Henrik, and dove his snout into the hot, delicious food.

As he ate, Henrik amused himself by watching the Rubbslings laptop screensaver. It rolled through images of the fancy school gates, the fantastic and modern assembly hall, through to the old castle from the Barryland theme park ... **WAIT, WHAT?**

'*If you ever see us being legitimately excited about Nica Konstantopolous shoes, you know we're in trouble . . .*' The words rattled around his beary brain.

Henrik dried his paws on his belly fur and pulled out his cracked special phone for bears. He scrolled back through his photos to the album 'Barryland Fun '05'. And there in the background of a **SELFIE** with Flobster and Jimmy the penguin stood the **EXACT SAME CASTLE** that currently stood in Jamie's school.

'Nica Konstantopolous shoes! They're in trouble! I know they are! The school! **It's a trap!**'

Sarah and Dominic looked up, startled.

'That right there is an old castle we were going to use for the Barryland theme park. It never opened so only a few of us ever saw it.' Henrik opened the Rubbslings homepage, flicked through the school images and made natural angry bear noises. 'There!' He pointed with his bear paw.

'Henrik, what on earth are you on about?' said Sarah.

'I know I'm usually wrong because

I'm slow, but this time I really think I'm right. I think Barry has lured Jamie into **a trap!'**

He explained it again more slowly, as well as what Jenners had said about Nica's shoes. He watched as Sarah's face changed from confusion, to disbelief, **TO RAGE.** Now, if you think parents go mad when washing is left on the floor or rooms are untidy, when their children are in danger, you can times that rage by ten thousand. Even Buttons was joining in the rage, with threatening yet still adorable growls.

'If Glen harms ONE HAIR on her head I swear to . . .' said Sarah, clenching her fists as Dominic looked on helpless and useless. Just to remind you, Glen was what Sarah and Grandma called Barry Bigtime because that was his real name.

'Glen? What's that **grotsack** done this time? Have they found him? Throw away the key, I say,' said Grandma, who had wandered in, wearing giant sunglasses and dragging a flowery suitcase, ready for her big cruise with Ethel. Sheamus the pig was following glumly, as pigs weren't welcome on cruises.

'Oh, Mum, he might have Jamie
and the girls. Henrik thinks they're in trouble.
The school, it was all him!' said Sarah, her hand
shaking. 'I'm calling Detective Lansdown immediately.'
She paused. 'But do we know where the school actually
is?' she added. 'When I looked up the address they
gave us I couldn't find it. I assumed it was a mistake. I
asked Jamie to send me the correct one . . .' She broke
off in a sob.

'I know someone who may know,' said Henrik.

'Who?' said Sarah with panic in her voice.

'Well, whenever we needed stuff for schemes and
things, we'd always get Bruce Burrell to deliver them
by balloon,' said Henrik.

'Oh, I can make Bruce talk,' said Grandma,
leaping to her feet. 'Known the boy for years. Know
his weaknesses. Come on, Henrik. We can deal with
him.'

'But, Mum? Doesn't your cruise leave this evening?'
said Sarah, who had no more capacity for problems.

'Don't you worry about me – **I've got a plan,'**

said Grandma. 'Sarah, you go and see that handsome police officer and while you're there tell him to answer some of my DMs. Leave the rest to me,' the old lady said with a wink.

CHAPTER 24
SUBJECT DAISY

Barry had grown tired of the castle's standard go-kart offerings so had gone off-road, smashed through the track entrance and was driving down the corridor, praying for someone to be wandering in his path. *This could be more fun if I had some paintball things*, thought Barry, and power-slid around the corner and—

'**WAAHAHAAAH!**' shouted Slottapuss, who dutifully took the hit like a champ. 'Nice hit, boss,' he said, staggering to his feet. 'I bring really good tantrum-avoiding news!'

'This had better be the best news, Slottapuss, as I'm in the sort of mood that may end with someone being marinated and fed to a beast of the **snapping** variety!' grumbled Barry, observing the hole in the castle wall.

'The best possible news, boss. Just got off FaceTime

with Flobster. Who's just had a Zoom with Proudy. Subject Daisy is in the Cliffside Camp with no visible defects and we have full control of her brain,' said Slottapuss proudly.

BARRY'S EYES LIT UP.

'And she's completely unaware?' said Barry excitedly.

'Yep. No awareness whatsoever. We planted a thought in her mind that Barry Bigtime may actually be innocent, and look at what she's posted!' said Slottapuss, showing Barry the video of Daisy tearfully spending eight minutes suggesting there might be a conspiracy against Barry Bigtime started by TV executive Gregorius Megacleese.

Barry danced a little jig.

'The only bad news is that our student followings are only on five hundred and forty-two million followers, so we may have to postpone the school-wide **Brain Hack . . .**'

Barry pressed a silencing finger against Slottapuss's rat snout. 'We press on, Slotty. We haven't a moment to lose. Five hundred and forty-two million followers is plenty. We need to control Jamie McFlair's brain before she starts poking her nose in. Commence Operation **Ultimate Brain Hack** at the . . . what is it we're doing?'

'A boxing match, sir. Between two of the top creators; everyone in the school will be there. And everyone is **VERY** excited.'

'I hate the internet,' spat Barry. 'Everyone who watches that nonsense deserves exactly what they're getting. What's the status of the apparatus?'

'The robots have been hard at work and we have produced more than enough Ultimate Brain Hack headsets. We'll give them out to students, telling them it's part of an immersive augmented reality experience, as opposed to taking control of their own minds. Everyone in the school will be wearing one.'

Barry thrusted with rhythmic delight. 'Slotty, you disgusting genius! Put the plans in place; we'll hack the brains during the main event! I'll prepare the rollercoaster.'

'You know we don't actually need to use the roller—' Slottapuss began.

'Silence!' Barry shouted. 'I want to use it when we steal Jamie McFlair's brain. **Only the best for my grotsack niece . . .**'

CHAPTER 25
THE BALLOONATIC

Bruce Burrell stood and admired his handiwork and added a balloon shaped like the letter G to his masterpiece. His evening's work was complete.

HAPPY 90TH BIRTHDAY GRAMPY ALAN FROM ALL THE FAMILY AND RUSTY THE DOG

It was spelt with fifty-seven individual shiny foil balloons and filled his entire shop.

Bruce wrote out a card advising the family not to let the recipient hold all the balloons at one time for they may **TAKE OFF** into the sky and end up in space. Bruce had learnt his lesson after the last time he lost a balloon recipient to space. His mind was about to drift off to that fateful night at Billy Clarkson's sixtieth when suddenly **A BIG, BROWN, FEZ-WEARING, FURRY BEAST BURST THROUGH THE BALLOONS.**

Bruce almost filled his underpants with products of fear and toppled backwards over the till.

'Waaaah! What on earth?' he said, peering over the till. He looked up and saw the crinkly but determined face of Grandma behind the bear.

'You were always a soft boy, little Bruce!' said Grandma, who could remember this particular Crudwellian from the days when they could both go through the whole night without needing a wee.

'Mabel!? What the blazes is this? Is that Barry's old bear?' said Bruce.

'We haven't got time for small talk,' said Grandma, tipping over a rack of balloon-ride leaflets. 'We've come here for information.'

Henrik limped closer to the till and helped Bruce to his feet and dusted him down with his bandaged paws. 'Hello, Bruce, long time no see! Look, this is really important. A friend of mine is in big trouble at Rubbslings School for Creators and Influencers. I

think Barry Bigtime is involved. We need to get to the school to make sure my friend is OK, and nobody knows where it actually is. **But I'm pretty sure you know.** So please tell us, Bruce.'

'I don't know what you're talking about!' **STAMMERED** Bruce.

The bear was so friendly, but it was still a massive bear. 'Never heard of such a school . . . Sure you don't mean Crudwell High?'

'He's a liar,' said Grandma, who picked up a mug of pens from the till and tipped them on the floor. 'Always has been . . . Oh ho!' she said. 'What's this, then?'

She bent over into the pen-y mess and picked up

one particular item that caught her attention. On the side of the pen in bright letters was *Rubbslings School for Creators and Influencers*.

'N-n-not sure how that got there!' stammered Bruce.

'Bruce, you should really tell us where this school is,' said Henrik.

'I won't talk!' shouted Bruce.

'I've got ways of making him talk,' said Grandma threateningly as she reached into her bag and pulled out a long, sharp knitting needle.

'Restrain him,' ordered Grandma, pointing the needle at Bruce.

The stocky balloonist was more suited to long distances rather than sprints and couldn't move fast enough from Henrik's firm but gentle restraint.

Bruce trembled as the sharp point of the needle in Grandma's jittery hand wobbled in front of his face before she jabbed it hard into a balloon.

BANG!

Bruce gave a gasp. 'Oh no, please. Not the balloons!'

'Talk!' said Grandma fiercely.

'Come on, Bruce, you've got to talk. She'll keep popping them – you know she will!'

BANG!

'No, please!' said Bruce.

BANG!

'I can't!'

BANG!

'OK, OK, OK!' said Bruce. 'I'll talk. I'll talk.'

CHAPTER 26

DETECTIVE LANSDOWN 2 - TOP OF THE COPS

Detective Lansdown was in his office on the fifth floor of the police station overlooking Birchester high street, reflecting on what had been a very solid day of **CRIME SOLVING.** He looked down at the civilians in his care. *Best be behaving yourselves tonight*, he thought. As tonight was the big policeman's ball. He observed himself in the mirror and straightened his dicky bow. *Haven't you aged well, old boy?* he thought, admiring himself in the mirror and **TWIDDLING HIS MOUSTACHE.** *It wouldn't be a party without a special treat, though, would it?* He crept across his office to the secret area where he kept his special things, like food he didn't want to share with the other members of the police force and snacks his wife wouldn't allow him to have.

Hanging proudly on the mahogany walls of Detective Lansdown's office was a portrait of Her Majesty the Queen. The detective listened out for approaching footsteps and gave the nose of the portrait a press. The painting swung forward, revealing Lansdown's secret refrigerated stash.

Behind the bottles of **CHOCO MOO JUICE** was a tall bottle of delicious party juice and, just as the detective's fingers were about to clasp the neck of the bottle, there was a loud knock at the door.

'JUST A MINUTE!' Lansdown shouted, flapping to get the painting closed as the door opened.

'Everything OK, sir?' said Detective Dubbs, whose own detective senses detected suspicious behaviour.

'Yes, fine I was, just you know . . . putting on my detective-ball slacks,' said Lansdown unconvincingly.

'Sure. Anyway, bit of a situation,' said Dubbs, striding over.

'Oh for crying out loud, can't these people just go three hours without playing up?' **HUFFED LANSDOWN,** who had been looking forward to the policeman's ball all day.

'Sarah McFlair is here. She wants to speak to you. Says it's **urgent.** Got some intel on the Barry Bigtime case.'

Lansdown sprang into life on hearing this information. He hated an unsolved crime. The unsolved nature of the Barry Bigtime case had been doing his head in for quite some time. It was up there with the mysterious disappearance of Olivia Wilbraham's mobility scooters.

'Well, what are you waiting for, man! Send her in!'

Sarah McFlair entered the office, brimming with mothersome worry. Lansdown offered her a seat, thought about offering her party juice, deemed it inappropriate, so told Detective Dubbs to fetch her a tea. He sat down and opened his notebook.

'How can I help you, Ms McFlair? My colleague says you have something to tell us about the **Barry Bigtime case.**'

'Yes, thank you,' said Sarah as she took the tea from Detective Dubbs. And regaled everything she had heard from Henrik as Detective Lansdown and Detective Dubbs scribbled everything down.

'. . . The bear said this,' said Detective Lansdown as **HIS FACE FELL.**

'Yes, but . . . you know Henrik, Leroy. You know he's not a false bear.'

'No, but he's a **talking bear** with human ears who wears a fez and a waistcoat. Who, by the way, is supposed to be a secret, Sarah. That was part of the deal for him not ending up in a zoo,' said Lansdown.

'He thought they were in trouble!' said Sarah.

'Yeah, but tales of bears in suburban villages aren't normally associated with peace and quiet,' said Lansdown, imagining the stress that widespread knowledge of Henrik's existence would cause him.

'What's that got to do with any of this?' said Sarah impatiently. 'Why aren't we doing something now? **What's the problem?'**

'The problem I have, Sarah,' said Lansdown

calmly, 'is that for me to act on this, I will need to get the green light from my superior. If he's going to sanction a potential international manhunt, he's going to want to know where I got my information from. And I can't in good faith tell him that this is based on the word of a talking bear.'

'But I'm telling you, Leroy! You've got to help us, Jamie's in trouble!'

'They'd have my badge! They'd think I'd lost my marbles,' said Lansdown.

'Just tell him I told you, Jamie McFlair's mother!'

'Unfortunately, Ms McFlair,' drawled Detective Dubbs, 'I've written down, *and the bear said that he recognised the school castle from the one he built in a defunct theme park.* And when it's in the notebook, Ms McFlair . . . can't rub it out. **Police rules,**' said Dubbs apologetically.

'So there's nothing you can do?' said Sarah desperately.

'Unless we get some evidence provided by

someone who isn't a talking bear, our hands are tied,' said Lansdown.

'SIR!'

Another detective – who, if you're interested, goes by the name of Detective Procter – burst into the office.

'Have you not heard of knocking, man? What's wrong with you?'

'Urgent call, sir. Just got a call from Bruce Burrell's Balloon Emporium. Reports of **a bear on the loose** on Crudwell High Street. Last seen trying to get into an old lady's limousine.'

CHAPTER 27
TUNES IN COSTUMES

The Goggly-Eyed Cheeseburger stood centre-stage, its true identity about to be revealed to the nation, as the *Tunes in Costumes* crowd started to erupt.

'SHOW YOUR FACE!' chanted the crowd, desperate to find out which celebrity had been singing in the giant cheeseburger costume.

'SHOW YOUR FACE!' screamed Nica Konstantopolous, who looked deranged as she stood over the judging desk, her large hair bouncing and her dark brown eyes bulging.

'SHOW YOUR FACE!' yelled her fellow judge Tyler East, who was standing on the desk. Both his massive arms were fist-pumping wildly.

'Show your face?' said Scott, trying not to laugh. *What is this show?* he thought. *It's even more ridiculous than* The Big Time. The other lads in BNA were going to think this was hilarious. He'd been told by the producers to take the face-showing ceremony very seriously.

Two men in shades and tuxedos entered the stage and started to slowly lift the goggly-eyed cheeseburger bun, revealing a sweaty old man with silver hair. *I literally have no idea who this man is. Sorry to this man*, thought Scott.

'OH MY GOODNESS, IT'S JEREMY GRIBBLES!' yelled the host, Will Kelly.

'JEREMY GRIBBLES!' squealed Nica.

'YES, MY MAN GRIBBLES!' shouted Tyler.

Who's Jeremy Gribbles? thought Scott . . . But his brain told him to follow Nica and Tyler's lead.

'JEREMY GRIBBLES! MY FAVOURITE!' shouted Scott, clapping **ENTHUSIASTICALLY.**

The crowd looked confused and disappointed but applauded all the same, and after a brief chat with Will Kelly, Jeremy Gribbles sang one last song half-dressed as a cheeseburger.

'CLEAR!' shouted the floor manager to signal that

Tunes in Costumes was off-air. Scott bounded to the rail that separated the audience from the stage, took some selfies with some fans, thanked the hard-working studio crew for their efforts, **FIST-BUMPED** Tyler East and made a quick happy birthday video for one of the cameramen's daughters.

As you can see, Scott's happiness was restored when he and the other members of BNA stepped back into the **BOYBAND GENERATOR.** Some say their talents returned, and then some. Scott had never been happier, Harrison's hair was even longer, Beck's voice never sounded smoother and J had never had more balance. He waved to his bandmates, who were supporting him from the VIP area. BNA had skyrocketed to superstardom. The only downside to all of this was having to take a weird medicine every morning at 6.30 a.m. The talking bear had been quite adamant about taking the medicine and, after seeing boys turn into monsters before his very eyes, he didn't dare argue.

Scott got to his dressing room and flopped into a fluffy, purple armchair. He was about to google who

Jeremy Gribbles was when there was a knock.

'Come in!' said Scott cheerily.

'Sorry to disturb you, Scott . . .' said an underpaid TV minion. 'But there is a mad old lady and a bear here to see you . . . I don't have a bear on the costume list, but he seems friendly enough. The old lady is out of control. Should we call security?'

'No, don't call security,' said Scott. 'If it's the old lady and bear that I think it is, it's cool, I know them. She gave me a lift in a bus last year. **It's a long story.** Which you probably know. Because it was in the news. But yeah. Send them down!'

Scott was confused. Why were Jamie McFlair's **MAD GRANDMA** and the friendly but also quite mad talking bear in the former BigTime Studios?

The door burst open as Henrik bundled in, shortly followed by Grandma.

'Henrik! Mabel!' said Scott. 'Bring it in, guys – what are you doing here?'

The three of them had potentially the weirdest group hug in history and Grandma brought Scott up to speed.

'Knowing Barry, he'll have some security of some sort as well as Flobster and Slottapuss, presumably,' said Henrik, stroking his chin. It was amazing what his brain could accomplish when his friends were in trouble. It was like a panic monster in his head had scared his brain into working properly. 'We're going to need some numbers, though. Do you think the rest of the band would be able to help us?'

'**Absolutely,**' said Scott with no hesitation. 'Jamie risked her neck to not only save our careers but pretty much our lives. I'll give them a call?'

'No time to lose, then!' said Grandma with a wink.

Scott and Henrik, with Grandma under his arm, sprinted through the television studio as Scott had one of the most bizarre conversations of his life with his bandmates.

'Yeah, meet me, the bear and the old lady by the white stretch limousine.' It was a sentence that was almost too absurd for books.

When they got to Grandma's limousine, the engine was running. Another old lady was at the wheel.

'Scott, this is Ethel. We picked her up on the way,' said Grandma. 'Watch her, she's feisty.'

Harrison, J and Beck arrived at the limo, already giggling at the ridiculousness of their lives.

'More young men? Like all my Christmases at once, this! And I've had quite a few Christmases!' cackled Ethel.

'In you get, chop chop! We've got a boat to catch!' shouted Grandma.

'A boat?' said Harrison.

Scott threw a glance to the other members of BNA. *This is probably why other bands have managers*, he thought, *so they know what they're signing up for*. Still, he put his immediate concerns to one side; there was no questioning that their band owed Jamie and her friends more than just their success.

Once everyone was in the limo, which to be fair was actually the most practical-sized vehicle for this very specific situation, Grandma explained her **MASTER PLAN.** Making bonkers plans seemed to run in the family.

'So it's Ethel's cruise-holiday vessel that we'll be commandeering. They needed a last-minute entertainment act and, thanks to Ethel and her persuasive ways and past love affairs, BNA will officially be joining the crew as **on-board entertainment,** Henrik is their costumed backing dancer, and Ethel and I are the warm-up act. You'll also get all-inclusive wristbands once we get on board.'

'Free food and drink!' cheered Harrison.

'GROTSACKS!' exclaimed Grandma. 'We might have a problem here – text from my daughter saying you've been spotted, Henrik, and I should've never let you leave the house, apparently. **Very bossy, isn't she.**'

'I'm not being put in a zoo,' said Henrik nervously. 'They don't even let you cook your own meals!'

'RIGHT, ETHEL, STEP ON IT!' yelled Grandma.

'Seat belts on!' Ethel screeched as she accelerated directly over an upcoming roundabout and on to the bypass ahead, to a jarring symphony of car horns and shouts of 'MANIAC!' by enraged road users.

As they powered down the bypass, it wasn't long before the flashing blue headlights of Detective Lansdown's supposedly undercover crime-busting car appeared behind them.

'Been a while since my last car chase,' said Grandma while simultaneously clutching on to J, who got carsick on journeys to the supermarket so was really out of his depth. Ethel accelerated, pinning her passengers to their seats.

'We really need a manager,' said Beck, full of terror, and the BNA boys all agreed that would be the number one priority when this vehicle came to a complete stop.

'Lose him, Ethel!' squealed Grandma.

Ethel swung across the road, slamming the brakes on, which swung the back end of the limo precariously up on to the pavement as she navigated corners at speed. Despite her terrifying but quite impressive driving, there is a limit to how much weaving you can do in a ten-metre-long stretch limo.

'I THINK I'VE SHAKEN HIM,' hollered Ethel.

'HOW LONG LEFT?' yelled Grandma.

'DESTINATION IN THREE MINUTES,' Ethel yelled back, partly because of the noise of the traffic and partly because neither of their hearing was too great in their golden years.

As they reached the harbour, Ethel veered off the road, rumbled over into the taxi lane and screeched to a halt.

'Quickly now, Henrik, give me and Ethel a hand, will you.' Henrik, who was a little more immune to car chases from his evil henchman days, hopped out and hoisted up Ethel and Grandma in each of his bear arms and began **SPRINTING** at pace to the cruise ship docked up in the harbour. The BNA boys clambered out and followed suit not far behind.

'HURRY!' yelled Henrik, pointing a paw at the arriving blue lights of Detective Lansdown's car.

The detective had burst out of his car and was in hot pursuit of Team Grandma, who were blending into the queues of jugglers, dancers and alternative sea entertainers who were about to also set off on an ocean voyage.

Henrik popped down the elderly ladies, who promptly hustled their way to the front of the queue.

'Hi there, we're here for on-board entertainment, terribly elderly we are, have our designated assistance team with us, this one here and those four handsome young chaps are performing, guests of Captain Roger, we are,' Ethel unloaded on to a nervous-looking, spotty boy who was ticking off names on a clipboard. 'Oh, also,' she went on, 'we seem to have a slightly, erm, "keen fan" following us, who won't leave us alone, just so you're aware.'

The boy at the performer's entrance of the cruise shuffled nervously. His elderly-person training kicked in immediately. 'Uh . . . right . . . yes of course, ladies, come straight in, hold on to the rail there. Love that your fellow entertainer is already in costume, already in the spirit.'

Henrik nodded at him and began walking slightly more rigidly to try and make out that he was indeed a convincing costume. Scott thanked the attendant and ushered the BNA boys in.

It was a full two minutes before Lansdown caught up with them, severely out of breath. Much of his detective work was computers nowadays so his fitness levels were below par.

'Excuse me, excuse me, Detective . . . Lansdown,' he panted, pushing his way to the front of the queue of people boarding.

'Detective Lansdown,' he said as he reached the spotty boy, fumbling for his police badge in his pocket. 'I'm in pursuit of an elderly lady driving a stretch limo and a bear with human ears.'

The queue of entertainers began laughing under their breaths.

'Sure you are, **Mr Crazy Fan.** I was warned

about you. I'm afraid, sir, I'll need you to step aside,' the boy said, wafting Lansdown away with his clipboard.

'I'm an authority of the law, young man! There's a dangerous elderly lady on the loose.'

The crowd laughed a little louder this time.

'Sure there is. I'm afraid without any form of ticket I cannot let you on board; it violates a string of fire-safety regulations, not to mention we're leaving shortly and you don't seem to have any proof you're a **REAL** policeman.'

'IT'S IN MY POLICE CAR!' yelled Lansdown in frustration, pointing at his undercover crime-busting vehicle.

'Doesn't look like a police car to me, sir. I'm going to have to ask you to leave,' said the boy.

'Do not let this boat leave!' said Lansdown in a voice that sounded calm but was clearly full of rage as he trotted off at pace back to the car.

Sweating and red-faced from both running and rage, he rummaged through the documents and Choco

Moo Juice cartons in the front seat of his car.

'No, no, NO!' he yelled before spending a further ten minutes emptying the entire contents of his glove box before finding his police badge in the coat he was already wearing. The cruise ship sounded the horn again as it pulled away from the harbour in the distance. 'NO, NO, NO, NO, NO!' Lansdown shouted, falling to his knees a little dramatically.

Lansdown scanned the pier. Towards the other end stood a sign: *Wesley Warren's Wavy Watersports*.

'Plan B,' he muttered under his breath.

CHAPTER 28

CHOOSE YOUR FIGHTERS

Jamie woke up on Saturday morning full of nerves, knowing that today could be the day she would once again come face to face with her uncle Barry. Jamie checked Daisy's social media accounts. Her posts filled her with dread that Daisy had somehow lost her mind, but also relief knowing she hadn't been harmed. Her videos had been getting more and more bizarre: 'Barry Bigtime for President', 'He Never Knew About the Monsters' and, perhaps worst of all, her latest video, 'How to Make Barry-Bigtime-Themed Cupcakes'. Jamie pulled herself together; she needed to focus on the task at hand.

The entire school was **BUZZING** for the boxing showdown. Every student had posted their predictions on who would be facing off. The fighters were to be announced in the morning and the fight to take place that same evening.

'If we don't care about the match, why do we need to go to the fighter announcement?' grumbled Jenners, kicking an empty can of Guggleschrumpf down the corridor. 'It's either going to be Jeremiah500, Samurai or probably one of the Larsson brothers,' she said, listing the boys who would strut down the corridors like they owned the place. 'Plus we're not even going to see—'

Jamie put her fingers to her lips. They were all forbidden to talk about the plan.

'—see . . . anyway, because we'll get rubbish seats,' Jenners quickly corrected herself.

They sat down on the cold marble floor, which was something their bum cheeks never really got used to, as Al G Rhythm appeared on-screen. *How did I not realise the Barryness before?* thought Jamie. Having to sit around on an island with Barry potentially metres away made her **SKIN CRAWL** since finding out from StompyDog. But they had no choice. They couldn't do anything that would raise alarm until it was time.

'OK, GANG, THE MOMENT WE'VE ALL BEEN WAITING FOR! OUR BIGGEST CREATORS WILL FACE OFF IN THE MAIN EVENT OF OUR BOXING EXTRAVAGANZA! BUT WHO WILL IT BE?'

Jenners gave a large yawn.

'IN THE RED CORNER WILL BE... WITH 8,986,542 FOLLOWERS... **SABRINA GUMBEAR!**'

A cheer rose up around the auditorium, and Jenners's interest perked up. 'Cool that the girls are in the main event!' said Jenners. 'Mum would be all over that.'

Even Jamie's brain released a few excited chemicals to swim among the anxious ones. The thought of Sabrina Gumbear getting pasted in a boxing match was particularly delicious. It was a shame she wasn't going to be around to see it.

'IN THE BLUE CORNER WILL BE... WITH 8,994,910 FOLLOWERS... **MELISSA GRAINGER!**'

Jamie and Jenners looked at each other in horror. **'WHAT?!'** they both shouted.

An even bigger cheer rose up, as Mel was super popular.

After the announcements were over, Jenners and Jamie barged through the crowds to try and speak to Mel, who was being carried on the shoulders of a group of Class 500K+s as they sang, 'Ooooh, Mel-i-ss-a Grainnnger,' to the tune of a popular guitar-riff-based song.

Further down the corridor, also being held aloft, was Sabrina Gumbear. Around her, another group of Class 500K+s were performing a choreographed dance routine.

'This is BAD news,' said Jamie.

'Mel's not going to go through with this, is she?' asked Jenners, thinking about her wheezy friend who became cross-eyed at loud noises and feared old ladies. 'Sabrina will destroy her.'

'She hasn't got a choice, but what about the plan!? Mel's in the main event! They're not exactly going to let her sneak off, are they? She's going to be surrounded by the security robots, teachers, students . . .'

'You reckon Barry's done this on purpose, Jamie? Knows we're on to him?'

It's the exact sort of thing Barry would do, thought Jamie. She shut her eyes tight, trying to think of a solution.

'Jenners, remember when we watched your mum in that wrestling match and when she was beating up that person, their friend ran in and sneak-attacked her?'

'Yeah, Mum was annoyed about that for ages,' said Jenners.

'Maybe you need to do that for Mel. Just be there ready in case she gets in trouble.'

'But what about you?' asked Jenners.

'I'm with StompyDog. I'll go with him, follow his plan to take down Barry. You stay at the fight and make sure Mel is OK. I'll be fine,' said Jamie.

They pushed through the crowd to get to Mel. Jamie knew that participating in the main event of a school boxing match was Mel's worst nightmare multiplied by massive numbers. She liked feeding the ducks and sometimes going for outdoor walks. Zero per cent of her genetics were designed for boxing matches.

'MEL!' yelled Jamie and Jenners together, from outside the doors of the 500K+ common room, desperately trying to get her attention as students thrust phones in her face.

'Sorry, just a minute,' said Mel to the crowds as she pushed through, not wanting to be rude but already exhausted from the attention. She looked like she was about to have a **MELTDOWN** before going within five hundred metres of the ring.

'I can't do this,' said Mel, hiding her sad eyes under her sunhat. 'I didn't mean to get picked! I've ruined the plan! I'm going to lose badly, I know it!'

'HEY,' said Jenners with purpose. 'That is not the attitude of the certified **monster slayer** that I know as Melissa Grainger.'

Jenners lifted up Mel's sunhat and looked her dead in the eyes. 'I'm gonna be with you; I'll find a way to be ringside and if it looks like you're in trouble, I'm getting involved. It's in my DNA; I've been training for this my whole life,' Jenners said, grabbing Mel's hand, just as a crowd of Class 500K+s grabbed her other hand and dragged her away, chanting.

*

Jamie spent the rest of the day in her room, going over every possible scenario she could think of. *Will Slottapuss be there? What about Flobster? Might Barry have a whole group of people on his side?* She felt sick with nerves. Later that evening, she loaded up her slime blaster, packed some supplies into her rucksack, took one glance at the photo of Henrik and Buttons and made for the main school building.

Jamie climbed the stairs to the upper tier seating. 'GET YOUR # T E A M G R A I N G E R HEADSETS! GET YOUR #TEAMGUMBEAR HEADSETS!' shouted the merch sellers.

The queue for headsets was **MASSIVE.** 'They won't let you in without one,' grumbled a streamer to Jamie as she tried to walk past the queue. 'Apparently there is an augmented reality experience and you need the headset to enjoy it.'

Jamie rolled her eyes, grabbed herself a **#TEAMGRAINGER** headset and strapped it round her head.

Jamie sat alone at the back of the Class 0–10K seats. In a reverse to assemblies, the Class 0–10Ks were now right at the back of the assembly hall, which was ideal for when she had to sneak out. She tried to spot Jenners, who was trying to sneak her way into the ringside Class 500K+ seating area, so she could jump the barrier should Mel find herself in trouble.

The lights in the assembly hall went down to 'ooh's of the students, and intense drum and bass rattled through the arena. Jamie looked at the arena clock. It was time to leave.

She sneaked out of the hall and into the upper corridors and opened her bag. She stuffed the

#TeamGrainger headset inside and replaced it with her Kid Ninja hair band, tying her red hair back into a tight bun. In her bag were some spy items she'd had to fashion like the olden days. A broken bit of mirror stuck to a coat hanger with a piece of gum so she could look round corners. An old watch. And her trusty **SLIME BLASTER.**

She peeked through the railings and down to the floors below to try and spot any patrolling robots. No sign. She made her way down the stairs and into the main corridor. She tried the doors. Locked. Had they all been trapped inside the main school building? There had to be a way out somewhere. She scanned the room until an idea buzzed into her head. On the far right door to the main entrance, there was a flap for the influencer dogs. Luckily, it was wide enough for Jamie's wiry frame to squeeze through.

The outside air was cold and a light breeze swept through her hair. She looked around for any sign of anyone outside and was suddenly startled as the dim hum of BNA's 'Friends Like Us' rumbled from the school building. Mel must be making her entrance. She had to hurry to find Stompy, try to take out Barry and shut the school down before Mel got hurt.

'What took ya so long? One minute late by my watch, kid.'

Jamie jumped in surprise and turned to see Stompy next to her.

'Sorry,' said Jamie. 'It's only me. Jenners is making sure Mel is OK in the match.'

'Come on,' Stompy said. 'We gotta get to the castle.' He nodded in the direction of the beach.

The castle looked even stranger in the **DARKNESS OF THE EVENING.** The odd towers and corridors poking out at strange angles gave it a monstrous look.

'Such a dumb, ugly building,' said Stompy, scanning into the building. 'Stay close; the rat thing and the lobster dude will be in here somewhere. So be on your guard.'

'I'm good,' said Jamie, pulling out the slime blaster. 'I've taken Flobster out with this before.'

'Nice!' said StompyDog. 'I feel an awful lot safer with Jamie McFlair in tow, that's for sure.'

They stepped into the castle and Jamie felt a chill wash over her. It was like stepping back into Barry's mansion. It even smelt oddly similar, whiffs of piercing fragrances and odd food.

'We need to take out the two goons first,' said Stompy. 'Follow me; there's a room where we can **upgrade** our tools!'

They came to a thick, heavy-set door that Mr StompyDog heaved open. It was full of a chemical smell, strange masks and paintball guns.

'I've left some supplies in here for us,' said StompyDog, handing Jamie a **PAINTBALL BLASTER** and a mask. 'I replaced the paintballs with a little extra ingredient that will take care of the rat and the lobster. Nothing lethal, though. I am a vegetarian, after all.'

Stompy pulled out his phone. 'Hey, Flobster, Slotty. You guys about?'

'Hey, Stompy. Yeah, we're just about to watch the fight on Slotty's phone. But there's a big girl in the ring causing a fuss – not sure what's going on.'

'Never mind that, you two, we've got a situation. Just had a tip-off. Jamie McFlair is in the castle – she's in the pottery room. Get yourselves in there **now!'**

StompyDog hung up the phone and gave Jamie a wink.

'Stay back here, kid. I'll handle this,' said StompyDog. Down the other end of the corridor, Jamie saw Flobster and Slottapuss barge into a nearby room.

I'm Jamie McFlair. I've got this. The memories of Barry had seeped back into her brain and started a fire in her belly. She was here to get Daisy back and she would not be cowering round corners or wasting valuable time.

'Hey!' whispered Stompy. 'What are you doing!?'

Jamie moved out into the corridor and stealthily followed Slotty and Flobster inside the room.

'Where is the **nauseating little worm?'** said Flobster slowly, his antennae twitching alongside Slottapuss's nose.

'Nauseating worm? Bit rich coming from someone who looks like a posh person's leftover dinner,' said Jamie, standing in the doorway, paintball gun in one hand, slime blaster slung over her shoulder.

Flobster's beady eyes swung round first, followed by his grotesque crustaceous body, his claws snapping at pace.

SPLAT, SPLAT, SPLAT. Jamie got one straight in his eye.

'ARGGHHHH . . . GET HER, SLOTTY!!!' screamed Flobster.

SPLAT, SPLAT.

Jamie unloaded another round into Flobster's mouth as he tumbled to the floor, claws flailing in the air.

Slottapuss darted straight at Jamie, his arms open wide, ready to grab her off her feet.

'Come here, you **VERMIN,**' he yelled, a line that he was more familiar with hearing than saying.

Jamie held her nerve for just a second longer before diving head first through his legs, expecting to slide through the other side and have him cornered. Instead, she felt a thin, furry hand clasp around her ankle.

'GOT YA, you 'orrible little pest,' said Slottapuss, spinning around and launching Jamie like a shot put across the room. Jamie smashed against the shelves opposite, causing a cascade of Barry-shaped clay pots to come clattering down all around her. Jamie's head was thumping in time with Slottapuss's footsteps stomping closer to where she lay. She kicked off the rubble that lay on top of her and pointed the paintball gun at the rat beast who was looming closer into view.

Click click.

She tried again.

Click click.

OUT OF AMMO.

Jamie used all her strength to roll on to her front as Slottapuss's fist smashed into the pots where she lay. She rolled over again, this time swinging the slime blaster from over her shoulder into her hands.

SPLAT, SPLAT, SPLAT, SPLAT.

She took no chances, peppering
Slottapuss with thick goo that sealed his eyes
shut and sent him into a tumbling spiral, crashing
into a set of shelves that rained more terrible Barry
pottery on top of him as he collapsed to the ground.

Jamie dusted herself off and climbed to her feet.
Her head was throbbing and her arm bleeding.
StompyDog burst into the room and took in the
scene.

'What the . . . ?'

'Pottery incident,' said Jamie. 'Where. Is. Barry?'

'This way. Come on, kid, we haven't got much
time,' said StompyDog, who for the first time sounded
a little nervous.

After a longer sprint around the snaking corridors
of the castle, they came to the largest set of doors that
Jamie had seen so far.

'This is it,' said Stompy. 'This is where Barry has
been hiding his new machine.'

Jamie gulped. 'Is he in there?' she said, still not sure
how she'd feel coming face to face with her uncle

again. All sorts of emotions were starting to surface. She had so many questions. Most importantly she wanted to talk to him. *Why does he do the things he does?* Years and years of sending people mad with promises of fame and fortune that ultimately only benefit him. Driving people to become literal and metaphorical monsters.

'Come on, Jamie, I need to know you're ready to go through with this. Don't bail on me now, OK?' said Stompy desperately. 'I've been working a long time for this and I need you with me; **we're going to take this guy down together.'**

Jamie switched her mind to Daisy; she did not leave friends in trouble. She nodded as StompyDog tapped the lock to the room with his phone and the large doors creaked open.

The room was gloomy. Jamie squinted into the darkness. There was something large in the room. She stepped over what looked like a train track to get a better look, slime blaster raised. Her eyes moved to . . . **A TEACUP RIDE?** She jumped as she noticed a person sitting in the teacup.

IT WAS DAISY.

Jamie, full of relief to see her friend, dropped the slime blaster and ran over to give her a massive hug.

'I'll deal with the console,' said StompyDog, running to the Ultimate Command Console podium.

'Daisy! I'm so sorry about before, are you OK? I think Barry may have scrambled your brain or something . . . Is this a new machine? . . . Daisy? Daisy . . . Hello?'

Daisy wasn't responding. It was like she was looking through Jamie.

'Mr StompyDog, what's wrong with her?' said Jamie. But before she could get an answer, Daisy had **GRABBED HER.**

'I'm really sorry about this, kid,' said StompyDog, who was punching commands into the console.

'LET ME GO!' Jamie screamed.

'Take her to the car, Daisy. Make sure she's wearing Brain Hack headgear.'

Daisy dragged Jamie, kicking and thrashing, up a

long ramp that led to a rollercoaster car, decorated with her uncle Barry's sneering face. Jamie struggled but she was already feeling the effects of her pottery house showdown with Slottapuss and Flobster.

StompyDog pulled out his phone. 'Hey, Barry, buddy. Get yourself down to the machine room, my man. **We've got a situation.**'

Jamie's heart sank and she couldn't have felt more stupid and alone.

CHAPTER 29

CRUISING FOR A BRUISING

Henrik had never been inside a cruise ship before. In fact, technically he was the first bear ever to set sail on the open seas, although that was not a record that anyone had kept track of before. He looked around the crammed cabin of old ladies and boybands. He was excited by the prospect of adventure with some of his closest friends, which for once wasn't headed up by an **EVIL MUSIC MOGUL.** He felt much more comfortable on the side of good and owed a lot to Jamie for ultimately saving his life. Entertainment also seemed to be his calling as elderly ladies and kids alike waved at him ferociously on board the ship, assuming he was some sort of sea mascot.

On Saturday morning, Grandma, Ethel, Henrik and BNA gathered in the foyer at the staff meeting point.

'Right, I know we're all new to this, but we know what we're here to do.' Grandma proceeded to hand out a schedule to everyone.

'Actually . . .' Harrison, BNA's drummer in the band, who spoke with a Northern twang, raised his hand. 'If we are commandeering this boat, which I'm already quite anxious about, why do we need to be putting on a show?' he asked.

'Ah yes, well you see, last time I tried to take over a naval vessel, long time ago, I had much more hair, almost as much as you . . .' Grandma went on. 'What I learnt is that it's much more straightforward if nobody on board knows you're doing it, until you're at the helm. **Timing. Is. Crucial.**'

The BNA boys looked concerned.

'Terrible trouble if all the passengers find out halfway through – people overboard, alarms raised, scramble for the lifeboats, that sort of thing,' Grandma said.

Scott, Beck, Harrison and J all gulped in union. 'So basically, we're the distraction?' asked J.

'Right you are!' replied Grandma. 'Drag out some of those catchy songs of yours for as long as possible and maybe throw in a few olden-day ones, just so people can actually sing along.'

'I feel used,' **MUMBLED BECK.**

'If my timing calculations are correct, we will reach the location that balloon boy gave us by nightfall,' said Grandma, handing out napkins covered in scribble. 'Now then, don't leave this schedule lying around, whatever you do. As you can see, we are all to arrive at the stage door at 4 p.m. Ethel and I will get into our outfits because we're on first; we'll get the crowd warmed up with our loveable personalities. Then BNA boys, you come on to rapturous applause. Henrik will support you as your backing dancer.'

'We don't usually have any backing dancers . . .' said Scott nervously.

'Trust me, it's what your fans never knew they wanted,' Grandma assured, as the other boys raised their eyebrows in various different directions.

'All clear?' asked Grandma.

Everyone **NODDED AWKWARDLY** in agreement.

The group, who despite probably not asking enough essential questions at the initial meeting, were all on board for the right reasons. They studied their handouts and agreed to meet back at 4 p.m. Any slight confusion as to what Grandma meant by Henrik 'stealing the show' was clouded by her pointing everyone in the direction of the entertainment deck.

As it turns out, cruise ships are full of fun potential distractions, many of which Henrik was seeing for the first time.

'I chose red and then black and then red again, and then the man gave me a big tower of circles, everyone was clapping, then I went back to the buffet AGAIN and then sat in a massage chair,' he said, as he popped on a fabulously outrageous headdress and other interesting garments that were in the backstage area. It's probably important that we describe this scene in more detail because it is quite something. Henrik was wearing a bright yellow traditional samba headdress and matching pair of shorts. He'd recently watched a documentary about a festival in Brazil and was always happy to learn. Truth be told, he was enjoying dressing up. Grandma and Ethel were wearing full Lycra one-pieces with colourful frilly sleeves. We'll spend less time describing that in detail. However, there was one thing for sure: everyone looked **FABULOUS.**

Grandma peered out from behind the curtain; the cruise auditorium was nearly full. *Perfect*, she thought. *Almost all of the passengers attend the opening show because they are overexcited on their holidays.*

She took a deep breath and gave a little nod to the BNA boys. 'Right, Mabel Coco Godzilla,' (which was what Grandma called herself on stage) 'let's be having you,' she whispered. She and Ethel, stage name just **'ETHEL',** waited for their cue and strutted out to rapturous applause.

You might expect two people in their eighties not to be a great comedy double act but you would be very wrong. In fact, they were smashing it. By the end of their five minutes, the room was full of belting laughter and excitement as the ladies welcomed the headline act.

'BNA, featuring special guest, back-up dancer bear!'

Grandma spun on the stage and gave a little nod to signify it was time for BNA and dancing Henrik to take over. She strutted down to the front of the stage, passed the rows of seating to shouts of 'Marvellous!' and 'I'm so ready for a boogie!' and out of the swinging auditorium doors.

Once they were clear of the audience, Grandma and Ethel shuffled down the corridor, grabbed their coats, which they'd left ahead of time, and stepped into the lift.

'Well done, old girl!' said Grandma.

'We've still got it haven't we? I don't feel a day over eighty-four.' Ethel did a little twirl in the lift.

'Right, focus – you ready for Stage 2? Time to visit an old love interest,' said Grandma with strong side-eye emoji energy. The pair giggled as the lifted dinged at floor five.

Grandma and Ethel skulked along the ship's corridors up to the control room. Being arguably the most important part of a ship, the room was sealed by two heavy-duty and supposedly old-lady-proof security doors.

'Right, this is the spot – it's all you now, Mabel,' said Ethel as Grandma got down on the floor and began to fake a leg-based injury.

'Oh no!' said Ethel, projecting her voice with her best acting skills. 'An elderly friend has had a fall.' Ethel waited, then looked round the corner, saw a member of staff and then repeated the whole performance again.

A young gentleman turned and came sprinting towards the ladies. 'Oh my goodness!' he gasped. 'Let's get you to the medical room straight away.'

'There's probably a full medical kit in the control room, I imagine,' said Ethel knowingly.

'Yes, of course,' came the reply as the man **SCANNED HIS KEYCARD ON THE DOOR,** which slid open, and began to help Mabel to her feet.

'Now!' shouted Ethel and as she did so, Grandma leapt to her feet, grabbed the keycard from the man, barged past him with Ethel and slammed the 'close' button on the other side, sliding the first door back across.

The man who'd thought he was coming to their rescue, but instead had been dragged into an unexpectedly elderly gang's plan, stood flabbergasted on the other side of the glass. One security door down, one to go.

CHAPTER 30
HIDING IN PLAIN SIGHT

Barry was about to burst into the **ULTIMATE BRAIN HACK** room but remembered the doors were sliding so had to wait.

Trapped in the rollercoaster car, all hooked up to the Ultimate Brain Hack, was a yelling **JAMIE MCFLAIR.** It was the first time Barry had seen his niece since the World Music Festival. His fists bunched with anger. Barry looked at her frightened little face. After everything she'd put him through. After stealing his house, crushing his reputation, here she was, trapped and helpless.

Stompy was standing at the Ultimate Control Console, and Daisy was peeking over the rim of one of the teacups. 'Here you go, Mr Bigtime, sir. Would you like to do the honours?' Stompy said, holding out the big red mallet that would spring the Ultimate Brain Hack to life. 'It's a big one. This will

320

start Operation Ultimate Brain Hack and everyone in the school will be under your control. **Congratulations, Mr Bigtime.** You've earned this.'

Barry giggled. 'This will be the cherry on the cake! I've been waiting so long to do this!'

'Well, let's get this show on the road!' said Stompy. Jamie struggled to try and break free of the coaster car, as the enormity of Barry's deceit became clear to her. *Control our brains . . .* She thought of Daisy's pro-Barry blog. *Clearly this mad machine actually works.* The thought of Barry being in control of Mel, Jenners and Daisy's brains enraged her. The thought of him controlling her made her feel sick.

Barry danced a jig. He couldn't believe it. He remembered being desolate in the roflcopter with Slottapuss and Flobster, planning the diamond heist, desperately hoping that the technology would make the **ULTIMATE BRAIN HACK** work. And it had! He looked over the Ultimate Command Console, which would control the most influential brains in the world.

And now for the final delight. Dealing with Jamie McFlair . . . He picked up the big red mallet. He drew it back. He turned to his niece and—

SPLAT.

Barry felt a sharp pain in his back.

SPLAT.

He turned around.

SPLAT, SPLAT, SPLAT.

Jamie looked on, stunned. StompyDog had shot Barry with his paintball blaster!

'What on earth are you doing, man!' stuttered Barry.

Stompy opened Jamie's bag and emptied its contents. Found the #TeamGrainger headband and pulled it on to Barry's stunned head.

'Gregorius Megacleese was right about you, Barry,' said Stompy as he grabbed Barry and dragged him towards the coaster car. 'He knew you couldn't be trusted. **He knew you'd mess this up.**'

Barry writhed. 'Take this off my head at once. You—'

'*BWARK!*'

From behind a teacup flew Gregorius Megacleese's blue-and-gold parrot, Beakers. It landed on StompyDog's shoulder. Barry froze.

'Oh yes. Remember Beakers? Gregorius has had his eye on you from the moment you stole his diamonds eight months ago. **Not quite as smart as you think you are, Mr Bigtime.** He knew of your plan to bring influencers to the island, so he came to me. Paid me quite a hefty sum to keep an eye on you. Who would suspect? Hey hey! It's Mr StompyDog!'

Barry began to wriggle once again, struggling to free himself from StompyDog's surprisingly strong grip.

BONK.

Barry's writhing and wriggling came to an abrupt halt as Daisy boffed him on the head with the big red rubber mallet. StompyDog hauled Barry all the way to the coaster car and squidged his body next to Jamie, pulling down the restrictive shoulder harnesses.

Jamie was furious about being tricked by Stompy. He seemed to have taken control of Daisy, so the machine must be controlled by the console. *Whose side is Stompy on?*

Stompy skipped back to the console. 'This whole thing was almost up in smoke because you underestimated Jamie McFlair. Again. Just like Mr Megacleese said you would. Jamie had you figured out. If it wasn't for me, she would have taken you down again. Which is why you shouldn't really be trusted with this.' Stompy tapped on the **ULTIMATE COMMAND CONSOLE.**

'So thank you, Mr Bigtime, for providing Mr Megacleese with the world's most powerful machine and the control of the most powerful influencers. He will be most grateful that you put his diamonds to such good use. As a little thank you, I'm going to gift Mr Megacleese access to *your* brain too, Mr Bigtime, if that's OK with you.'

Stompy picked up the big red mallet, and smashed the Jamie-faced button. With a loud *ding*, the coaster car began to move and the Ultimate Brain Hack sprang into life.

CHAPTER 31
COMMOTION ON THE OCEAN

'Come on, come on, come on,' muttered Grandma impatiently, as the furious man whose keycard they'd stolen banged his fists on the door.

'There!' shouted Ethel.

Around the corner, up ahead, came the faces first of Scott and Beck, then J and Harrison, who looked severely out of breath, and Henrik, who was still wearing his headdress.

The staff member slowly turned around to see the five of them sprinting directly at him. 'Oh, you have got to be joking,' he said, raising his hand in the air as a feeble attempt to stop them. The four BNA boys slowed down and let Henrik past and as he approached the first door, he scooped up the staff member in his arm and held him aloft.

'WHAT IS HAPPENING?' The man flailed,

confused at how such a convincing bear mascot was dressed so fabulously and also appeared to be unbelievably strong.

Grandma slammed her hand on the button from inside, which sent the door sliding open as the gang piled in.

'I'm really very sorry, sir, I'm sure you're a lovely man,' said Henrik politely, tossing the man back into the corridor, as Grandma hit the button to slide the first door closed and secure the area.

'Knew you had it in you,' said Grandma, relieved. **'Everyone OK?'**

The gang nodded. 'The audience were getting restless when we left, though!' said Scott. 'They were shouting for an encore and we just legged it.'

'Ethel, you ready for Stage 3?'

'I mean, it's been a little while but he won't have forgotten me, that's for sure.'

Grandma and Ethel held the keycard up to the next set of doors, which led to the control room and the control panel of the ship. The light above turned orange for a few seconds, waiting for the captain to approve entry, before turning to green and the door sliding open. Grandma and Ethel **CREPT IN** first.

There, sitting at the helm of the boat, looking out of the concave glass, among at least fifteen screens of dials and the beeping sound of the ship's radar, sat Captain Roger with his back facing them.

'Able Seaman Matthew, everything OK back there?' asked the captain.

'I prefer **First Officer Ethel,**' came the response.

Captain Roger immediately swung round in his chair as Ethel walked over to him, in full Lycra.

'Oh my . . .' said Captain Roger, who'd briefly misplaced all of his words. 'Er, glad you made it on board. Wait . . . how did you get up here?'

'Oh, I have my ways,' said Ethel, winking.

You may at this point be noticing a

bit of awkwardness between Captain Roger and Ethel and you'd be right to think so. This was Ethel's twenty-eighth cruise in total, the last four of which had all been under the helm of Captain Roger, who had taken quite the shine to her. Ethel, not wanting to tie herself down at the youthful age of eighty-four, had not quite committed to their relationship as much as Roger had hoped, but he still had a **SOFT SPOT** for her.

'What do all these dials do, then?' asked Ethel.

'Ah, well . . . lots of very complicated numbers and measurements. The boat is actually on autopilot for most of the time with today's modern gadgets. This screen is where you pop in your co-ordinates and then I just monitor speed, code and conduct of the sea . . .'

'I'm really sorry to do this, Roger. I do hope you'll forgive me,' said Ethel.

'Do what?' he replied as Grandma launched out from around the corner and wrestled him off his chair to the ground.

'What on earth are you . . . doing?' he blabbed as Grandma tied his hands together with J's bandana.

'You can't be serious!' yelled Captain Roger. 'You're crazy, what are you doing this for!?'

'Look, we can't explain right now, but we're rescuing my granddaughter and stopping my really very irritating son from causing some serious problems,' said Mabel as she began trying to work the autopilot screen. 'Now where do I put in my co-ordinates . . .'

ALARM ALARM ALARM.

The entire room filled with red as lights above flashed repeatedly and blared out an almighty siren. Grandma glanced over at Captain Roger, who'd slid himself across the floor and had pressed his back up against a big red button.

'WELL, THAT WAS SILLY, WASN'T IT!' yelled Grandma above the noise. **'HENRIK, GET**

IN HERE!'

Moments later Henrik trotted in, his paws covering his big human ears to protect them from the incessant blaring of the alarm.

'I SUGGEST YOU TELL US HOW TO TURN THIS OFF BEFORE I SET THE BEAR ON YOU,' Grandma screeched as Henrik felt a flashback to his Barry days – some traits certainly ran in the family.

Captain Roger looked completely terrified as he sat metres away from an actual real-life bear, who was still dressed quite absurdly and seemed to be obeying the elderly lady's every command.

'Er . . . there's an override switch next to you, Ethel . . . Yes, pull that . . .' he stuttered.

The piercing alarm noise and red lights stopped flashing.

Grandma breathed a sigh of relief. 'Good, right, don't do that again. Now, you're going to go on the intercom here and tell everyone that was a routine fire drill. Then you're going to show me where to enter my co-ordinates, understood?'

Captain Roger **NODDED FURIOUSLY,** while not breaking eye contact with Henrik as he shuffled over closer to them and punched in the co-ordinates.

ONE HOUR UNTIL DESTINATION.

Grandma looked at her watch. 8.42 p.m. *Plenty of time to save the day.*

CHAPTER 32

THE DEBT OF GREGORIUS MEGACLEESE

It was 8.43 p.m. and the rollercoaster car began to judder forward as Jamie desperately tried to haul herself free.

'Uncle Barry, wake up! We have to get out of here!' she yelled at her woozy uncle. 'Daisy! Daisy! You have to snap out of it!' Jamie yelled as her friend blankly looked on. '**You have to remember!** Remember Queen Gnome! Remember Jenners doing Sassy Monkey! Remember BNAaaaaahh!' The coaster car flew down into the darkness of the Barrymouth.

'ULTIMATE BRAIN HACK 33 per cent complete,' said the console. There was a loud crash and in bolted Slottapuss, covered in dust and swaying with confusion.

'What's going on in here?!' the rat said, as Jamie

McFlair and Barry Bigtime emerged from Barry's own bottom in an explosion of confetti.

The explosion snapped Barry awake and he gave a wail – 'HELP, SLOTTY! DO SOMETHING! HE'S STEALING MY BRAAAAAAAIIIINNN!' – as the car started **WHIZZING AROUND** with the teacups.

Slottapuss charged at StompyDog but was blocked by brainwashed Daisy, who was still holding the big red mallet. Slottapuss had a system to deal with little girls. Unfazed, he picked Daisy up and slam-dunked her into a trash can, which wasn't quite big enough for girls, so she was stuck fast.

'ULTIMATE BRAIN HACK 50 per cent complete.'

'Uncle Barry, is there any way to stop this machine?' pleaded Jamie as they spun.

'There is only one way. The emergency override switch! Stops the machine, resets the Ultimate Brain Hack, but oh goodness, we will be under his control by the time we ever reach it,' moaned Barry uselessly.

'ULTIMATE BRAIN HACK 62 per cent complete.'

Slottapuss looked at Stompy and twirled the mallet. But just as he took a step forward, a blaze of blue and gold smashed into his face, knocking off his sunglasses. **'BWARK!'** shrieked Beakers as he flapped his metal wings in Slottapuss's face.

'ULTIMATE BRAIN HACK 74 per cent complete.'

'Where's the switch, Uncle Barry?' shouted Jamie, frustrated at her uncle's pathetic-ness.

'It's in the coconut shy, **of course!** Knock over the second coconut from the left, and it will stop the machine, but we'll never get there in time!'

Jamie, using all her might, struggled and kicked out at the rickety old rollercoaster car. As she struggled, she could feel the harness start to budge. No wonder they'd never passed a single safety test. With one last push, she had just enough room to ease her wiry frame from under the harness. As the teacups began to slow, she leapt from the coaster car, throwing her headset to the ground.

'ULTIMATE BRAIN HACK 86 per cent complete.'

Slottapuss, fuelled with rage that his designer shades may be scratched, managed to catch the mechanical parrot by its tail feathers and **FRISBEED IT ACROSS THE ROOM,** where it whizzed over Jamie's head and hit the wall with a squawk and a crash. Jamie, who was still dizzy from the teacups, tried to get the room into focus. A non-dizzy Jamie wasn't very good at throwing. What was she going to do?

'ULTIMATE BRAIN HACK 98 per cent complete.'

Ninety-eight per cent?! She was never going to make it. But lying in the gloom was her trusty slime blaster. She ran, scooped it up, turned and had a chance to make one shot. She pulled the trigger.

The thick gooey globule of slime **FLEW ACROSS THE ROOM.** Jamie, Barry, Slottapuss and Stompy froze to watch. It was as if time stood still as the slime

blasted the second
coconut from the left
off its perch.

**'ULTIMATE BRAIN HACK
CANCELLED. ESTABLISHED BRAIN
HACKS WILL BE RESET.'**

'Ummm . . . guys? Why am I in a bin?' said Daisy.

StompyDog, in a very off-brand move, yelled a
number of things that would certainly get his YouTube
videos demonetised. Rage looked bizarre on his

friendly-looking face. His problems were about to get worse as Slottapuss was ready for battle and was taking big-boy strides towards StompyDog, rolling up the sleeves of his navy suit. With no mallet and limited paintball ammo, StompyDog assessed the situation.

There was no time. He would be no match for this rat beast. He had to cut his losses. Even without the influencers' brains, Gregorius Megacleese would find Barry's **ULTIMATE BRAIN HACK** machine VERY useful. He grabbed the console and, using the podium as a springboard, managed to hop over the charging Slottapuss. Stompy grabbed Jamie's discarded headset, and **SPRINTED FOR THE DOOR.**

'SEIZE HIM! STOP HIM! THE ORB! HE HAS

MY PRECIOUS MACHINE!' wheezed Barry, still stuck fast in the coaster car.

Slottapuss ran to the car and, using his rat-monster strength, pulled the harness clean off its hinges as Barry flopped from the car with a wail.

Jamie was trying to process what had happened to her. She saw that Stompy had been using the console to control Daisy. She didn't know much about how the machine worked but knew that she couldn't let it be in the hands of bad people. **SHE HAD TO STOP STOMPYDOG FROM GETTING AWAY.** She would deal with Barry later.

Both Jamie and Barry sprinted through the doors after StompyDog with Slottapuss in tow. As they ran, Jamie and Barry looked at each other, both realising the strangeness of them now having the exact same goal.

Barry's poor chasing skills came back to haunt him and he began to tire, and Jamie's legs weren't long enough to keep up with StompyDog. They were going to lose him.

There was a rumble behind them, and as Jamie turned around, Flobster arrived at speed in one of the go-karts. **'Get in,'** he said.

Jamie, Barry and Slottapuss piled into the go-kart. Flobster couldn't have been more confused.

'Wait, if Jamie McFlair is here, who are we chasing?'

'JUST DRIVE! WE'VE BEEN DOUBLE-CROSSED – THAT MAN HAS STOLEN MY MACHINE,' roared Barry.

They zoomed after StompyDog.

'He'll be heading to the harbour,' said Barry. 'It's the only way he'll get out from here.'

Jamie was poised with her paintball blaster ready to take him down on sight. They started to catch up with him as he was reaching the archway that led down to the harbour.

Jamie fired some **PAINTBALL BLASTS,** as StompyDog returned some shots of his own. The first caught Slottapuss plum in the face, causing him to topple out of the cart with a crash. The second struck Flobster right in the antennae, which is a very sensitive

area for a lobster. Flobster swerved and **SMASHED** through one of the flimsy walls of the Barry Castle, tumbling on to the gravelly beach below. Flobster writhed on the floor, nursing his stinging antennae. Barry and Jamie clattered out of the go-kart as StompyDog ran towards a rickety pier. He jumped into a little red boat, fired it up and sped away.

'It's not over yet – grab that one!' yelled Barry, pointing at a motorised grey dinghy that did not look seaworthy. Jamie and Barry ran to it, climbed aboard and kicked the motor into gear.

'I'll DRIVE,' they said in unison, before Barry shoved Jamie off the controls and slammed the throttle down to maximum.

The boat bounced along the waves in pursuit of StompyDog, who seemed to be extending his lead at a **RAPID PACE**.

'USE WHATEVER'S ON YOUR BACK!' yelled Barry as he tried to dodge out of the way of the spray of sea-water.

Jamie's mind was in overdrive. StompyDog, her own childhood hero, had lied and then lied again and was escaping with a **DANGEROUS** machine. Now she was in the same boat as the man who had planned to do it all. *If Uncle Barry stops Stompy instead of me, then we're all back to square one*, she thought.

Jamie grabbed her slime blaster, knowing full well this was not the situation it was designed for. She loaded up a cartridge and fired it over the boat. It shot out at pace but fell abysmally short of StompyDog.

'UGH, YOU IDIOT. FASTER, FASTER, FASTER!' yelled Barry, putting all of his weight down on the throttle. He was losing StompyDog and any chance of reclaiming fame, fortune and Bigtime-ness in front of his own eyes.

'THERE'S NOTHING BUT OCEAN THIS WAY, STOMPY, YOU GROTSACK!' yelled Barry into the wind.

'Maybe he's going to Gregorius Megacleese!' shouted Jamie, raising her voice over the sound of the engine, remembering what StompyDog had told her while she was strapped in the rollercoaster car. Barry turned his head and **GLARED AT HER.**

'Who is he, Uncle Barry?' Jamie asked, desperately trying to force the puzzle pieces together in her mind while keeping Barry talking. 'Is he an enemy of yours?'

'He WAS a very close friend,' said Barry angrily. 'Back when I was as snot-nosed and irritating as you are. He owes me.'

'What does he owe you?' asked Jamie, desperately trying to stay calm as they were being flung across the waves.

'**EVERYTHING.** Neither of us would have anything if it wasn't for ME saving both our skins each and every day. Back when Lobber Livingstone used to hoist us up by the neck after school and shake us of all our money, steal everything we owned and then pass us along to Farnell Winterbottom, who'd bruise us until we were sore. Those two made every day miserable for us **FOR YEARS.** And they would have done for a lot longer if I hadn't acted! Came up with a little invention, I did . . . They needed to learn that you don't mess with Barry Bigtime . . . Anyway, ENOUGH questions if you know what's good for you. You're one shove away from **shark food** and I'm struggling to find a reason to keep you on this boat.'

Jamie said no more. But it was the most human she'd ever seen her uncle.

As StompyDog began to pull away in the distance, there appeared to be a shadow up ahead, which grew in size with every passing second. It was a dot at first but as they powered through the water, it grew larger and larger as it rose tall over the horizon.

StompyDog changed course to try

and avoid the impending wake of what was now clearly a gigantic cruise ship heading in their direction. On one side of the ship were eight bright-yellow lifeboats that appeared to be slowly lowering down into the water. Barry, who had his eyes locked on StompyDog up ahead, followed his exact path, uninterested in distressed holiday-makers.

As the yellow cruise-ship lifeboats touched the water, they disconnected from the main ship and began to head in StompyDog's direction.

'YES, YES, GET IN HIS WAY,' shouted Barry over the rumbling of the engine and splash of the boat against the sea. StompyDog changed course again, opting to go round the lifeboats and ignore their **CRIES FOR HELP**. Barry followed and they slowly approached the boats, close enough that they could begin to make out the faces of the occupants, one visibly much larger than the others on board.

As Jamie squinted her eyes and stared at the passing boats, hoping they weren't in too much danger, she made out the shape of the larger person.

'HENRIK!?' she yelled.

'HENRIK, IS THAT YOU!?'

For a rare split second, Barry took his eyes off StompyDog and glanced across to the lifeboats. He immediately swung the boat a hard right away from them, which threw Jamie off her feet, slamming her into the rubber side of the rib. She clutched on to the rope inside and steadied herself.

'LET HER GO, BARRY!' boomed Henrik's voice from the lifeboat, which was now struggling to keep up.

Barry laughed out loud. 'YOU PATHETIC EXCUSE FOR A HERO, HENRIK,' he shouted back.

'JUMP, JAMIE!' came a familiar shout.

Jamie wanted to leap straight off the boat. Even at the speed it was going, it would hurt but the pain would be temporary. She could float long enough for Henrik to collect her and— *Is that Scott? How?* Now she wanted to jump even more; she wasn't a strong swimmer but Scott would swim to her, she was sure of it. After everything she had done to save them, she was the helpless one now. Barry was making her decision for her as they powered on, leaving the lifeboats further and further behind. She looked back desperately and then back again to StompyDog. **THIS WAS NOT OVER YET.**

Where is StompyDog going? thought Jamie, *Is there anything even near here?* She wasn't sure exactly where they were but there was certainly nothing in sight as far as the horizon. The island where Rubbslings was was becoming smaller and smaller by the minute as they carried on into the open ocean.

'What's your plan?' shouted Jamie. She could see that StompyDog was increasing the gap between them every minute. 'We're not going to catch up with him!'

'You have NO say in this. Be quiet before you become shark fodder. I won't tell you again,' came Barry's reply, his eyes still focused on the target. 'Besides, you're the one with all the PLANS!' he yelled. 'Plans that are none of your business, plans you should've learnt to keep your grotty little n . . . OH, you have GOT to be kidding me.' Barry laughed in the sort of way adults do when they are not finding something funny any more.

Detective Lansdown was zooming across their path on a bright, purple speedboat. Something big and yellow was bouncing behind him in the water. He raised a megaphone.

'GLEN JONES, YOU ARE FORMALLY UNDER ARREST. PLEASE STOP YOUR VEHICLE IMMEDIATELY,' came the **BLARE OF THE MEGAPHONE.** Glen Jones was Barry's real name but it brought back bad school memories and 'Barry Bigtime' was much more grand and evil-sounding.

'They're a joke, LOOK at them!' Barry shouted, which to be fair wasn't entirely incorrect. Detective Lansdown had borrowed a banana boat from the harbour. Between boat and banana stretched a long rope that cut between the Stompy boat and the Barry boat.

'*BSHHH*,' came the sound of the megaphone. 'THE ROPE WILL TANGLE YOUR ENGINE.

WE REPEAT. BRING YOUR VEHICLE TO A COMPLETE STOP IMMEDIATELY.'

The other lifeboats surrounded Barry.

'MOVE OR I'LL RAM INTO YOU!' he yelled desperately.

'YOU WOULDN'T KNOCK YOUR OWN MOTHER INTO THE SEA,' yelled Grandma through the wind.

'MOTHER?!' shouted Barry, stunned.

'GRANDMA?!' shouted Jamie, also stunned.

Jamie threw herself on to the controls to stop Barry from trying anything rash.

'BARRY BIGTIME, YOU ARE COMPLETELY SURROUNDED. PUT YOUR HANDS IN THE AIR.'

'YOU CAN'T DO ANYTHING TO ME – I'M BARRY BIGTIME. I'LL HAVE THE LOT OF YOU . . .'

The end of Barry's rant started to get

drowned out by the noise of something mechanical, which increased in volume until it was the only sound either of them could hear. Jamie stared into the distance. A helicopter was flying towards them. **THE ROFLCOPTER,** Barry thought with an evil grin. *I'm saved*!

But then his smile dropped in disbelief as a sleek, black helicopter drew closer. It had two sets of propellers like one you might see in a war film, quite unlike Barry's run-down metal lump that had been his home for months before Rubbslings. Written on the side of the chopper in bold white letters was:

MEGACLEESE.

As it approached StompyDog, it lowered in height, and a man descended from it on a winch. StompyDog let go of the boat's controls and grabbed on to him, before turning to Barry and blowing him a kiss from the ladder as the winch retracted, taking both the men with it.

'NO, NO, NO!' Barry slammed his hands on the boat engine,

covering his face from the spray. All seemed lost. 'They've taken it. My life! It's gone!'

Jamie looked at him with disgust. **'YOUR life?** What about my friends' lives? All of those students who you tricked into another one of your awful plans with this awful machine. Which is now in the hands of whoever this Gregorius man is . . . It's not fair!'

'Pah!' Barry spat. 'Gregorius was never the smart one. He'll never work out how to use the machine. He, like everyone else, had no faith in me. But it doesn't matter. I am ruined. It was my only chance. And I've got nothing left.' A big sadness snot bubble exploded from his nostril and he broke down into a blubbering mess.

It was the sadness that he'd only allowed his face to show during the most private of times before he'd built Rubbslings School, and it took control of his body. Barry closed his weepy eyes and lay back in the boat, as if he were back in the marshmallow room. **HE'D LOST ALL HOPE.**

As Jamie looked down at him, her anger turned to

pity. It looked like it was finally over for Barry. *What made you so evil?* She felt like she was starting to understand.

The other vessels had closed in and Detective Lansdown leapt on to Jamie's boat. He slapped Barry in handcuffs.

'Mr Bigtime, I am arresting you on the suspicion of unauthorised monsterfication, falsified educational systeming and for making bad TV talent shows.'

Jamie couldn't believe it. Barry was finally caught. She looked in the sky, expecting the roflcopter to appear from the spray, or for Flobster to burst from the sea, but Barry was being hauled into Detective Lansdown's boat.

A big bear paw reached out to her as Henrik pulled her safely on to his lifeboat, where she gave him and Grandma **THE BIGGEST HUG IN THE HISTORY OF HUGS.**

CHAPTER 33

THE RETURN OF THE SASSY MONKEY

After Barry's arrest, Jamie, Grandma, Scott and Henrik had motored back to the beach and into Barry's room of stress-carnival rides. Daisy was sitting in a teacup, hastily deleting **EVERY VIDEO** she'd made while under the machine's control. As soon as she saw Jamie, she burst into tears and gave her a massive hug. **'I'm so sorry!'** she cried.

Jamie smiled. 'No, I'm the one who should be sorry. I shouldn't have said the things I did. We need to find the others. Mel was facing Sabrina Gumbear in a boxing match. I'll explain everything on the way!'

The group raced back to the school and main hall where the boxing match/brain-stealing event of a lifetime had been plunged into confusion. Kids all throughout the arena lay motionless on the floor, exhausted from being forced to create an obscene amount of content for weeks and stunned that the most popular creator in the school had been attacked by a wild goose and then suplexed by a girl in Class 0–10K, **GRANTING MEL THE VICTORY.**

Jamie and Daisy sprinted straight into the ring, where Jenners and Mel lay next to a groaning Sabrina Gumbear. Jamie clambered on to the top ropes of the ring and cleared her throat. 'Everyone, there's something you should know . . .' She told them *everything*.

The four friends waited with Grandma, Henrik and BNA for the police to arrive. Some of the 'teachers' had tried to **FLEE** the scene, but escaping from an island with no form of transport was largely an unsuccessful pursuit. Most of them were so exhausted from swimming that by the time the police turned up they were floating in the sea like ducks at a carnival stall.

The cruise ship docked soon after and students were

returned home, while members of the boyband camp were given immunity from prosecution if they would give evidence against Barry.

Flobster and Slottapuss, however, were nowhere to be found.

Jamie was with the police when they rescued the missing students from the Cliffside Camp. Happily for them, their side effects seemed to have gone and they'd mostly returned to normal. Jamie was bemused to see one boy refuse to be parted from a microwave he was carrying, but forgot about that when Percival's beaming face came into view. 'Wow! Can't believe I've been a victim of a **Barry Bigtime** scheme and rescued by *the* Jamie McFlair!' he practically yelled.

'Nice to see you too, Percival.' Jamie laughed. 'I never thought I'd say this but I can't wait to get back to Crudwell.'

Barry was charged with crimes of brain stealerage and monsterfication, two laws they had to invent specifically for him. His name was once again all over the news:

'Barry Behind Bars for a Big Time', 'Brain Thief Arrested by Police Chief' and also one weird article about 'Strange Crushes You Love to Hate', where Barry came forty-second. Finally, it was over.

The girls hadn't uploaded much since getting off the island. Occasionally they'd have a quick scroll or group chat with Scott and the BNA lads but, at least for now, they'd decided that having four really good friends was better than ten million that they didn't really know. Besides, they were getting constant calls wanting to interview them on how they'd **TAKEN DOWN THE GREAT BARRY BIGTIME FOR A SECOND TIME.** As far as Jamie was concerned, the less time spent on Barry-Bigtime-related activities, the better, which at least for the weeks afterwards meant basically not going online. Maybe they'd do a group channel together in the future, but when they wanted to and because it would be fun, not because a mad Barry Bigtime algorithm told them to.

Two weeks later, they were back at the mansion and back in the marshmallow room. Jamie was relieved to be reunited with Buttons the pug and Mel relieved to be reunited with her **TROUBLESOME GOOSE.** The animals were snoozing with Sheamus the pig in a pile of softness.

'You'd definitely be Flamboyant Fox. Look at the way he moves; it's like you when you get a new fancy hat you like,' said Jamie, nestled between two large, comfortable pillows in the marshmallow room.

'I'm not that bad,' said Daisy, laughing, ejecting a mouthful of popcorn on to the floor, which Buttons immediately snaffled up.

'Mel . . . now who would you be . . . ?' said Jenners, pretending to be deep in thought.

'Don't!!' said Mel. A smile started uncontrollably taking over her face. 'I'll choke on the sweets!'

'SASSY MONKEY!' Jenners immediately leapt over to Mel, and began grabbing sweets out of her bag and gobbling them down. Mel crumpled to a quivering wreck, laughing uncontrollably in a heap.

'Stoppp . . . I can't even,' she said, struggling to

breathe once again.

The girls sat eating snacks, making each other laugh until their ribs hurt and generally speaking over *Animals With Attitude 2*, partly because they'd also seen this one upwards of eleven times and partly because the sequels are rarely as good as the first one – **THIS BOOK EXCLUDED,** obviously.

It had been a long time since Jamie had laughed so much without a little pang of worry in her brain, but with Barry behind bars and the machine destroyed, she had got back what she'd always wanted: her best friends.

'We still have to meet up every weekend,' said Jamie after Mel had stopped laughing and got enough oxygen in her lungs to carry on surviving.

'Nah, I'm gonna make new friends . . .' said Jenners. **'JOKING,'** she said, pointing at Jamie, whose face was laughing shocked emoji. 'Actually, I'm not totally joking, like I probably will also actually make some new friends. Maybe they can come round!'

Despite it being Jamie's biggest worry in the

summer, the girls going to different secondary schools was something that scared her much less now. The ordeal they'd been through had put everything in perspective and besides, there was plenty of time after school and at weekends.

'Yeah, definitely!' said Jamie. 'Only if they like BNA and *Animals With Attitude* and swear not to tell a soul about Henrik. Maybe it's better if we all go to one of your houses; we won't be here much longer anyway.'

Jamie let out a big sigh and slumped back into the marshmallow cushion. She would miss this room, to be fair.

Let's leave our heroes there. With her uncle Barry behind bars, Jamie could **FINALLY** relax. Well, almost – she couldn't shake what he'd told her on the boat, about being bullied as a youngster. Maybe this answered the question she'd had all year about why Barry did the things he did. Would this Gregorius Megacleese character ever work out how to use Barry's machine? But the most important problem had been solved, as she, Jenners, Daisy and Mel were reunited, slumped in marshmallow comfort, bellies full of delicious snacks, their friendship stronger than ever. If they could survive monster-fied boybands and a crazy school then they could definitely survive going to different secondary schools.

~~The End~~

CRASH!

'What was that?' said Jamie.

It was Henrik, who'd appeared in the doorway with a panic-stricken face.

'Haha, what is it?' said Jamie, who was used to Henrik's clumsiness by now. 'What did you break?'

'His promise to keep you safe,' came a voice Jamie recognised.

Out from behind Henrik, one claw firmly pressed against Henrik's back, **WAS FLOBSTER.**

Jamie sat bolt upright and blinked her eyes repeatedly. Her brain struggled to process what was right in front of her.

'HEY!' Jenners got to her feet.

'H-h-how did you get in?' stammered Jamie.

'We know this mansion like the back of our hands. Know all the secret, stinky, sewery entrances,' sneered Slottapuss as he emerged from the shadows. Mel was making a screaming face but **NO SOUND** was coming out; Daisy looked for something to throw but everything was made of cushion. Jamie snapped out of her brain fog and walked towards them.

364

'Let go of Henrik,' she demanded. 'One call to Lansdown and you'll both be arrested.'

'Ah ah ah . . . I don't think that's a very good idea,' said Flobster menacingly, clicking his pincer. 'For starters, wouldn't like to see cuddly old Henrik end up behind bars, now, would we?' Henrik tried to wriggle free but Slottapuss grabbed his arms behind his back.

'You see, we have a bit of a situation,' said Slottapuss. 'Mr Megacleese and Mr StompyDog are in possession of a Barry-Bigtime-flavoured machine called the **Ultimate Brain Hack.**'

'We know that!' said Jamie impatiently. 'But Uncle Barry is the only one who knows how to use the machine, and he's going to be in prison for a long time.'

Flobster laughed, clicking his free claw as he spoke. 'We all know your Uncle Barry isn't Man of the Year . . . but Gregorius Megacleese makes Barry Bigtime look like Father Christmas. With his money and connections, he'll definitely work out how to use this machine. **And that's bad for everyone,** let me tell you.'

Slottapuss shuddered. 'So if you know what's good for you, you might want to join us on a little visit to see your uncle. He *is* family, after all . . .'

'Why would we help you?' asked Jamie.

'Because we are now in a very similar unpleasant situation. We are all enemies of Gregorius Megacleese. Which is not good news. We stole his diamonds; you messed up his evil plan. Take it from someone who is an expert in evil plans: when someone messes them up, you want revenge. It's kinda just how things go on the evil side of the fence here,' explained Slottapuss.

'And you really don't want Gregorius Megacleese to reach your uncle Barry before we do,' added Flobster.

'So what do you say, Jamie McFlair?' Slottapuss said. 'Are you in or are you out?' He extended his disgusting furry hand.

Jamie's eyes darted towards her

friends. Their faces were etched with shock as Flobster clicked his pincers threateningly. She looked to Henrik, whose fez was wobbling with fear. She had to make a snap decision for everyone's sake. Jamie closed her eyes and **SLOWLY REACHED OUT TO GRASP THE HAND.**

ACKNOWLEDGEMENTS

It's important to say the biggest THANK YOU ever once again to our amazing editor, Mr Tig Wallace and the whole team at Hachette Children's (you are AWESOME and you know who you are). Also another shout out to the legend that is Davide, our illustrator who, as I'm sure you'll agree, has absolutely smashed it. His illustrations genuinely make us crack up and he does an excellent job at bringing the strange things that live inside our brains to life. And a final thank YOU for picking up this book and joining us on another wild tale. We hope you had an ace time and will join us for the next book!

Luke and Sean

Luke Franks and Sean Thorne are a debut author duo. Luke is a presenter on CITV's *Scrambled*, has presented *The X Factor* online and *The Voice* online, and is a Sony Rising Star award-winner. Sean is a presenter on the Fun Kids radio show, runs a successful YouTube gaming channel with 120k subscribers, and is a Nickelodeon Kids Choice Award nominee.

Luke and Sean met at university and have been creating comedy together ever since. They live in London and often co-walk a dog called Goose.

**ALSO AVAILABLE AS
AN AUDIO BOOK!**

ALSO BY LUKE FRANKS & SEAN THORNE

Jamie McFlair's favourite band just performed on the country's biggest talent show, but it all went terribly wrong thanks to Barry Bigtime.

Barry is a music big shot, all round nasty man . . . and Jamie's uncle. The next day, he launches his own massive new band and Jamie smells a rat.

There's something hidden in Barry's basement – a machine that is the key to his musical success. But what happens when the boyband generator goes wrong?